Simon Skinner

was born in Harlow, Essex, in 1966. He is a graduate of University College, London and his work has appeared in *Casablanca*, *Ego* and *Positive Energy of Madness*. He lives in London.

Song of the Suburbs

Simon Skinner

SKINN

First Published in Great Britain in 1998 by
The Do-Not Press
PO Box 4215
London SE23 2QD

A Paperback Original

ISBN 1 899344 37 3

British Library Cataloguing in Publication Data. A catalogue
record for this book is available from the British Library.

Printed and bound in Great Britain by The Guernsey Press Co Ltd.

h g f e d c b a

Acknowledgments

With a first novel there are a lot of people to thank, so lay readers should turn the page.

I'd like to thank my family for their support. Jim Driver for the belief. Martin Chalmers, whose efforts on behalf of my work have never faltered. Others who have gone out of their way to promote my writing include Matteo Sedazzari, Andy Walker, Valerie Byfield, Robin Tomens, Erica Christ. I'd also like to thank Matt Adams and Ju Row Farr, David Williamson, Dean Cavanagh, Paul Goodman, Simon Mason, Paolo Sedazzari, John Hardwick.

To Chuck

Girlfriends

The first time I came was outside French, a paved area between the language huts and the tuck shop. The school easy approached me and as had become our custom I welcomed her by sticking my tongue in her mouth and fondling her right breast. My friend who'd followed me out was disgusted with me, How could you kiss her? He exclaimed. I'm going to spread this round. I expect he would have been more shocked if he'd seen the small discharge of yellow spunk in my Y-Fronts. I didn't know what it was in the bathroom. I took a piss, thought nothing of it. I'd never masturbated as a child and so took the slightly queasy feeling I'd experienced as a commingling of pleasure, embarrassment and guilt. Later I caught up with my friend and dismissed the incident as horseplay. Little did he know I was going round there after school.

The girl wasn't attractive in the slightest. Her popularity was on account of her large frame and huge breasts, fully fleshed out at fourteen. In fact I recall she looked somewhat like a cow from distance. Kissing her was only pleasurable because she'd press up against you and touch you up. There was never any doubt of what was to follow if you had the courage to go round. She lived in the poor end of town by the supermarket. I cycled down there on my racer the first time. Not really expecting anything. Only knowing I was finally going to do it properly. I was sixteen years old. I'd lost my virginity to a virgin and the experience was fairly amateur. The easy I was now visiting, her best friend, a blonde who was fucking my best friend, told me all about the men and boys who visited her every night. I was just another. And it was the thought of how easy she was, how she had been fucked and fucked that was turning me on. I knocked on the door and her dad answered. I said her name and he pointed upstairs. Her room was plain, the bed unmade.

I wondered when you'd come round.

I want to keep this to ourselves, I said.

Don't worry Slim, she said, I won't spoil your little image.

She did all the foreplay. I was too nervous to blag my usual confidence. Those massive teats swaying in front of me. She was such a big girl I kept sticking it in her folds until she guided it in herself. I was hard enough not to worry about falling out and banged her like I'd not done the virgin. Afterwards I layed with her and sucked on her teats a while. She blew me off before I left and said I could pop round anytime. I nodded to her father as I exited. He'd been watching the football, cans of beer on the go the whole time.

Rape Girl

I was at a party held by a nicking apprentice of mine who was celebrating the mike and stand we'd managed to chore from the local concert hall. The girl in question was already very drunk by the time I got there fashionably/wankerishly late whatever you wanna call it. I'd never seen her at a party before but certainly I'd noticed her in the playground. She hung with squares and dressed like them, but the no make-up approach only enhanced her beauty. Long straight brown hair, always brushed. Her features delicate, with slim red lips and a cute little snub nose. She was a looker all right. Daddy's girl though apparently so no-one went near her. I guess she must have thrown off the shawls of parental pressure and got out tonight. Serious mistake. She was at that stage of drunkenness when vomiting wasn't going to help. She was either going to pass out or need a stomach pump. Fuck knows what she'd been drinking, some nasty cocktail of cheap Spanish wine and Cinzano no doubt. It was all any of us could afford. I stood there sipping on my Yager Lager and pretending to be above the young 'un who kept trying to get me outside.

She's out there, she kept saying, you can get to feel her up and she does nothing. Some of the boys are doing it, why don't you?

This little young 'un loved the fact that Princess virgin missy was getting her comeuppance. I figured I should take a peek. Sure enough, Missy was on her side, swaying between this world and the next and a couple of nasties were feeling her up, lifting and dropping her tidy firm breasts, sticking things up her etc and I went across and told them to stop.

Come on Slim, they said, don't be a spoilsport.

I tried to speak to her friend about getting her home but she had never been to a party either and gave me this strange blank look like she was stuck in Hell and did I have the password out.

All right do nothing then, see if I care. I wasn't that bothered.

I went off with my young 'un. We went upstairs. Coming back into the front room where music was blasting out and most of the booze kept, I saw Missy lying on the floor and the biggest guy in the school who wasn't cool but well hard lying on top of her and trying to slip down her dress. I admit the sight revolted me but I wasn't going to be the one to pull him off. I didn't leave the room either. I stood and watched as he hiked her knickers up. Ripped them. Did he rape her? I don't know. I saw the perfect brown of her pubic triangle and didn't want to see his huge swollen knob corrupting it. I went back upstairs. It was more like necrophilia than rape, she was slumped back in the style of a revived corpse. In the playground it went round of course, but as usually happens in these instances she changed schools and he never got done.

During those years two of my gang actually went to court charged with what would now be called date rape. Not for a second did we consider either guilty. Stupid cows, we thought, what did they expect going upstairs? There was no bruising was there? They just couldn't handle losing their precious virginity and daddy finding out. That's how we thought then. Every man for himself.

Brazilian Girl

You English are dead, she announced, dead. You won't call me tomorrow. All you care about is tonight. You just want to fuck me and that's it. A Brazilian man would never do that, you'd see him around and he'd become your friend, he'd invite you to meet his family, have dinner, he'd respect you even if there was no love, no relationship, he'd never treat me like this.

Instead of saying, yeah well we're not in fucking Brazil darling, I mumbled some drunken platitudes about the English having a more rarefied concept of passion, passion of the moment I think I said. At the word passion she nearly went into a dance. She dug out all her love letters from an ex-boyfriend and forced me to read them. I didn't but gave a good drunken impression of being able to read whatever language they were written in. Portuguese I suppose. Realising her mistake she took me over to her computer and zapped up the file in which she'd written a letter to this Swedish guy she'd fucked a few months back. The letter was disgusting, full of stuff about her getting wet and being able to smell it when he called on the phone and other things about her period I won't divulge.

Why are you showing this? I asked, bored now with her playing teacher.

I want you to understand about Passion, she said.

I sidetracked that little lecture by pointing at the family pictures on her wall.

Is that your family? I asked.

Yes, she said, relaxing a little.

I didn't realise your dad was black, I said, staring straight at the smiling polaroid.

He's not! She shouted, offended for some reason.

Who's that then? I pointed.

She let out a banshee scream.

You English, you care what colour my father is, no he is not black just because his skin is slightly darker than yours does that make him black?!

I was going to point out his negroid features but thought better of it and stuck to complementing the beauty of her mother.

Oh, she's beautiful right! Because she's white! Honestly you disgust me. You filthy English pig!

I poured her another whisky and she let me kiss her some more.

I picked her up at a literary launch party so I guess I should have been expecting some hysterics. She was staring straight at me most of the night, so after all the contacts I'd spoken to had gone, I went over and offered to buy her a drink.

The drinks are all free, she said.

Oh yeah, I said, thinking nothing of it and grabbing the barman. I got us two large ones. I was pissed enough to start kissing her pretty quickly, after about two lines of dialogue.

That's unusual for an Englishman, she said kissing me back, to be so forward.

How long have you been over here?

Don't you want to know where I'm from first?

Not really, I thought but quickly added:

Sure, Spain I guess.

Brazil, she announced triumphantly.

I suppressed a yawn. Really?

Later she returned to the subject of my perceived racism while cooking us something in the kitchen.

In Brazil we don't think like you English. We are all together. All colours. All mixed up, all living as one.

Really? I said using the cheese on toast to smother my smirk. Should get me out there for a few months, I said, soon change that.

If you went out there, she said, either missing my quip or rightly ignoring it, you could have any girl you wanted.

Why's that?

An Englishman, white, educated even if he isn't rich or good looking can have his pick of any number of beautiful Brazilian girls.

I thought you said there was no racism, I said.

How do you mean?

Well according to your theory even your sisters hold up the white race as some kind of gods.

I never said that, she said, the anger simmering in her again. I'm talking economic pressures. Reality! Wake up!

Yeah but I'm a good-looking confident guy. I could have my pick anyway. The fact that I'm white and English isn't really the point is it?

I was glad the question was rhetorical because that was totally the point. Anyway we went into a dark bedroom full of posters from English Heritage and the like and she had a full figure and showed no shyness under the duvet. I enjoyed the night of passion we shared even though my heart was cold and she was right, I had no intention of calling her the next day. I went through the charade of taking her number though, giving her a false one, getting on the tube, feeling a smidgen of guilt, laughing as I chucked the scrap of paper down a drain and stood there, as if I might watch it disappear. But London deprived me of even that much poetry, as soon as I threw it; it had gone.

German Girl

The German girl I met in Greece couldn't believe I stood her up on her last night.

I went to see *A Clockwork Orange*, I explained lamely. It's banned in Britain. I've only ever seen it on pirate video.

I shouldn't have added the last bit because it weakened my case.

Why couldn't you have taken me to see the movie? She asked.

I had no real answer. It honestly never occurred to me. Maybe somewhere in me I wanted to spare her the sight of me laughing along to the 'Singing in the Rain' rape sequence. When I was younger a friend conned me and some buddies into chipping in to a *Clockwork Orange* fund. I say conned not because the quality was shit or anything and not because I didn't watch it every time I went round there but because he got it on Betamax and all the rest of us had VHS. He got to keep the tape. As his parents were artists they saw nothing strange in the way every time they came into the lounge we were watching the 'Singing in the Rain' rape sequence. We especially loved the bit where Alex kicks wifey in the stomach repeatedly. We used to freeze-frame it. This friend also got a video camera for Xmas. The only ideas we had were to direct porn sequences with the village girls, or re-workings of the therapy scenes in *One Flew Over The Cuckoo's Nest*. We took it in turns playing all the patients; our performances outlandish grotesques of the original. The others all laughed but I took it oh so seriously. We made a film about rival gangs, but the dad showed he wasn't as liberal as he thought he was, and banned the camera after he'd seen a particularly good shot taken from the back of a scooter. He thought we were going to drop it! We were so disgusted at him we never made another film.

Anyway back to the German girl. I was supposed to follow her to another island but she was angry with me now and left. I'd met her and had to lie about my age anyway. She was confident enough to go topless and obviously about five years older than me but I'd had five o'clock shadow at fifteen and so could pass as her age range. She nearly caught me out once when I spoke of my older brother and having already mentioned his age, she stopped and said,

Older, did you say older brother?

Realising my lie I quickly took advantage of her stilted English and insisted,

Other brother, other not older!

Oh, she said not really believing.

I had such ability in those days. I kept a straight face and looked into her eyes without blinking. We kissed.

Underage Girl 1

She wasn't a virgin. She had a large nose, I remember having to swivel my head to kiss her. She was so small she had to stand on tip-toe even as I bent. I think she was fourteen and I was eighteen. As we went upstairs I pretended to be freaking out on scag so as to distract my friends on the stairs. Feeling ill? One of them shouted unconvinced. I lay on the bed, maybe because she was so young I held back. I'll leave it up to her, I thought. She asked what was wrong with me. I carried on the crazed junkie routine. This, perversely, made me more glamorous to her. A friend of my older brother's came into the room, saw me with her.

Like little girlies do we?

I was embarrassed but carried on with the sick act. You don't understand, she's my nurse, my student nurse that's why she's undressing me. She's my little pony. For years I'd run into this guy at similar parties and he'd say things like lock up your daughters or watch out he likes them young. For fuck's sake there was only four years between us! He looked like a YTS Fagin anyway so I took the piss back. Anyway the young 'un's got me undressed now and has climbed up on top of me. She was so petite she could balance her whole body on me without inflicting any discomfort. I said I wasn't feeling too well, wasn't really up to it.

Never mind she said, you'll feel all right in a minute.

Underage Girl 2

The other young 'un was a French girl who wrote me about twenty love letters after I'd returned to England. I don't know who gave her my address, but I used to enjoy reading them out on the playground for my friends to laugh at. She was table tennis champion and her parents were dance champions, outmanoeuvring all newcomers in the site disco. After her parents had won I reluctantly agreed to dance with her. The French Miss took me behind a post and we started kissing. I could see she'd fallen badly. I was about nineteen then I think. She was probably thirteen. She said she was fifteen. She had no pubes when I fingered her by the lake. A French family walked past and the mother of this group gave me the evilest look I've ever received.

I didn't take the finger out though. It was honey. I wasn't going to fuck this one, didn't want to. You're too young, I kept telling her but then she'd wait for my mother to leave our trailer in the mornings. Always the last to go to the pool before me, then the girl would knock on my bedroom window, get me up, cook me breakfast. On my last day she got in bed with me. I slept naked because of the heat and that morning had woken up with a hard-on, as you do. She mistook that as a sign and began to gobble me off.

The rest was just eventuality. I was furious with whoever gave her my address. Not because I didn't enjoy the letters, I just didn't want her father sending over the police/bill for an abortion/baby.

Teacher

She was helping me with my university entrance and corrected a couple of essays I had to write before my interview. She said my ideas were post-degree level, funny how they didn't share that view at university. I agreed to pop round her house after my interview, tell her how it went. I thought nothing of this at the time for it was the summer holidays, so why wouldn't I go to her house? It's incredible how naive you can be after so much experience. My sex-life with grown women was still fairly limited though, as limited as any other twenty-three-year-old. I went to the house and knocked on the door. The fact that she came to the door in tight trousers and boots, all made up wasn't particularly significant. She was always glamorous at college but it wasn't like I'd ever had a crush on her. I might have checked her bra-line in an idle moment but never payed any special attention. At no time did I ever think she was sweet on me until I sought her advice in the school holidays. She invited me into the lounge and the sight of her thirteen-year-old boy watching *Miami Vice* relaxed me totally. Not that I'd felt any threat, it's just in hindsight I can see why I was so unprepared for her. Then her ex-husband turned up. We'd just cracked open the champagne to celebrate my university acceptance when there was a loud banging on the door. A second earlier a small man with ginger hair and beard had pulled up in a Porsche. He gave me one look, she introduced me in a way that should have sounded off alarm signals but simply induced confusion (she introduced me like I was her boyfriend, not an ex-pupil), he gave her a cheque, didn't even look at his son, who didn't look round either, gave me a killer look which was pathetic, got back in his car and screeched off.

Why did you marry him? I asked, severely disappointed.

Slim, can you believe at one time I found him exciting?

We laughed together and knocked back the champers.

You are staying for dinner I hope? I've cooked a roast.

I know I should have gone then, that was my chance, my get-out clause, but I honestly felt sorry for the kid, he looked up at me with such a rueful expression I crazily concluded I had to stay for him! During the meal she plied me with wine and her son disappeared after desert. She spoke of the poetry she'd written as a student. I earnestly said I wouldn't mind reading some. Really? She said. It was the least I could do, I felt, after she'd waded through a year of my work.

My notebooks are upstairs. Do you want to see them?

Still nothing went off inside me. I followed her up, grabbing the banister to steady my drunkenness. I was on the bed with the notebooks in my hands when she placed her hand on my thigh. I got to admit, the sight of her fallen body wasn't too inspiring, but she knew how to caress a reluctant penis and so it went. Luckily my parents moved to France shortly after and I was installed in halls so the hounding phone calls which followed our one coupling stopped eventually.

Phone Girl

Speaking of phone calls, I had a girl call me every night at six forty-five for a year. If I answered she hung up straight away. If it was one of my family, she'd make them go and get me then hearing my voice hang up. If it was the girl I think it was, I'd not only slept with her but her sister as well. This girl hassled me for years to go out with her, until finally, as a joke, so she'd get the message (there was no fucking way!) I told her I'd go out with her if she lost two stone. Now as you've already read, I'm not sizeist against big women but this girl really pushed the margins. One day in class she asked for the window to be opened, complaining about the heat. Someone shouted out, What's the matter Louise, frying in your own fat? Needless to say we all laughed. Poor girl, although I could have done without the nuisance phone calls, but I guess from her point of view they worked. She got what she wanted eventually. After I'd made my infamous quip about her losing two stone, it got back to her and sure enough she went on this crazy diet. I'd get updates from her friends as if when she reached the magic figure I was somehow going to keep my promise! I did, but only on the intervention of her older sister. She was what Louise would have looked like if she'd reached the impossible target I'd set her. In other words no great shakes either. Both girls had Nordic backgrounds, were round-faced, had bushy hairstyles and were given to blushing. The older sister was nice enough but still no catch and I couldn't understand why she was getting involved.

I was in the library when she approached.

You know Louise is losing all this weight don't you?

Yes, I said embarrassed.

You still won't be interested Slim, will you?

I looked at her and thought no I won't.

You do know she's going to kill herself if you renege on the promise?

It wasn't a promise. It was a joke.

Oh and I suppose my sister's life's a joke as well is it?

No. Look you know me, I'm not into this diet bollocks, I'm just not interested, I don't care what she weighs, all right? She rings me every fucking night, and refuses to speak to me, I try to talk to her then, what am I supposed to do?

I was nearly in tears and stupidly, I now realise, I rested my head on her shoulder. Then the most surreal and unbelievable moment in this whole episode occurred. Older sister turned my head around and kissed me full on the mouth. She then put her hand in a place which can only be described as intimate. The shock and outrage I felt combined into one the stiffest hard-ons of my teens. She saw that, smiled.

Leave it to me, she said, and walked away.

At six forty-five the next night the phone rang. It was older sister.

We're in the bathroom, she said, right by the scales. Guess how much Louise weighs?

Don't fuck about, I said, I trusted you with this.

I know. Look, just come over. You know where we live don't you?

No.

I had to get a train, walk for a mile, ask directions, then I saw the house. What am I doing? Just walk away, I thought. I couldn't. The memory of that erection kept me going, I suppose, but I seriously thought I was going there to talk to Louise, talk her out of it. She'd nearly killed herself with this diet, I knew. I was also tired of the whole process and wanted this family out of my life. Older sister answered the door. Her hair was wet, her face flushed, she noticed me glance at the swell of her bosom beneath the orange bathrobe…

We both know why you've come round, she said. I followed her up.

Louise didn't kill herself but she began to get home earlier than her sister and wait for me to come round. In the little chats we had I got to quite like her and started seeing her as well. I'd be round there every night depending on who had detention or netball practise. I got to admit it was the excitement of fucking one and then the other which kept me going. In the end the older sister got home early, no netball, and caught me and Louise at it. She threw me out and I could hear them fighting as I walked away. Anyway I got my number changed in the end. Her older sister may have hated me and in the first place Louise, but it didn't stop Louise ringing me. I still get nervous if the phone rings at six forty-five.

The American Actress

If you go to London University you meet a lot of Americans over for a year. The college used to use them so they could give us homies full grants. English women friends of mine said I got involved with so many Americans because I knew they always be going home at some point. A sort of commitment-phobic safety net. Lisa looked like a blonde Julia Roberts. I don't say this with any particular pleasure, *Pretty Woman* isn't high on my top ten film list. She had the angular face, bee-stung lips, Bambi eyes. She was skinny, had long fountainous hair. She's the only woman I've dated whose beauty has stopped people in their tracks. Two examples: we were in a gay club, Heaven, on the supposedly straight night and some queen came up to her and said, I don't usually do this but I must commend your exceptional beauty. Thanks, she said. She knew how to take a compliment. She showered enough on herself. The other time was when we were in Cullens on Tottenham Court Road and a middle-aged woman with a trolley full of shopping stopped in the aisle and said, My word! She'd turned round to get a better look. I tagged along… I met Lisa at the read-through of *Macbeth*. She was one of the witches, I was Macduff. She was sat next to another actress I knew who was drinking a can of coke. I went over and asked for a sip. Finish it, she said, I don't know why I bought it. There was half a can left. For some reason I knew Lisa was watching me closely. I grabbed the can from my friend and emptied the contents in one greedy gulp, then I crushed the can, gave it back and returned to my place in the circle. Fairly bizarre mating ritual I'll concede but it did the trick. Lisa even noted the event in her journal. I didn't see her until the first rehearsal, I was busy seeing this mad Scottish fresher who kept taking me to boring art films at the ICA. After the Pasolini double header she'd apologise again and again, and I'd say don't worry and take her to some all-night drinking club. Anyway at the first *Macbeth* rehearsal Lisa and I showed off for each other and I made sure she knew we were all going to the Union after. In the Union she dug out her poetry notebook full of quotes she considered significant. I recognised a couple of the authors and we talked until last orders. I walked her back to her dorm across Russell Square and she told me about her first love she'd left back in the US. Well he's not here now is he? I said, trying to get an invite up to her room. She let me in for coffee and then read the journal extract I mentioned of our first meet. I took this as my cue. Went to kiss her. She turned her head. What about my boyfriend? Her look implied. Fuck him I thought, but settled for the old, Are you really going to stay faithful to him all year? Look you've only been here two weeks and you've already got an Englishman in bed with you. We were lying together on the bunk. Fine, she said, we can hug but not kiss. Fine I said. Eventually after about an hour of mutual appreciation we kissed.

The next morning her boyfriend rang and he was in tears at the other end when she told him about me. I was amazed at this. We hadn't slept together and never would but I guess you can't hide things from first loves. I left them to it, walked towards a café for some breakfast when I saw the Scottish fresher walking towards me… I quickly adjusted my scarf to cover the marks on my neck and had a little chat with her and her friend who'd just come down from Edinburgh. I arranged to meet her later but blagged a rehearsal I didn't have so I could fit Lisa in first. Most the time I spent with Lisa we just talked. She talked about herself mostly. She told me of her dream of becoming a great actress. She told me of how after playing Medea in a college production (nowhere grand just some muppet college in Iowa) the whole audience were so overwhelmed with emotion they sat in their seats stunned. No-one moved for twenty minutes. She was completely shameless in telling these stories. She told me the production we were currently in would be much improved if we were playing the leads. To be fair to her she was a good actress and had been shortlisted for Lady Macbeth whereas I was lucky to get any part in a Shakespeare production. My spontaneous jazzoetry style of reading blank verse hardly endeared me to directors. I don't know what happened to Lisa, she went to New York, modelled for Donna Karan, got into the Shakespeare Conservatory, left… then what?

Rich Girl

After her I dated a student whose father was Finance Minister for Saudi Arabia. I couldn't keep up with her. She even took black cabs to college. I went round to her flat once. It was the penthouse above her parent's palace in Kensington. I turned up in my ripped jeans and flying jacket and felt a little displaced. We took a cab to this restaurant and I said I'd take care of the wine. There wasn't a bottle under a hundred pounds. I was trying to survive on a grant at this stage. Later I played her piano, rather well I thought, but I'm not sure she really liked jazz. She said did I know any Satie and I said, put some on I'll pick it up. I could always play by ear and sure enough she put the CD on repeat and I stumbled my way through until after about the third go – I had it. She was amazed at this, amazed enough to lead me to the silken interior of her boudoir.

You are cultured then, she said, surprise in her voice.

FBI/God Squad Girl

Another American I dated was a friend of Lisa's. I payed her a compliment once and she never forgot it. Nor did Lisa, I had hell to pay later. Don't praise my friends in front of me! She shouted. I'd told her best friend Kathleen she had a religious face, I wasn't sure what I meant by this at the time but she turned out to be God Squad and blushed. She had a slight Oriental look, puffy skin above the eyes, long straight black hair which she later shaved off to get 'more into the spirit of London' (her words). She also had her nose pierced and bought DM's. I lot of Americans did this, and spoke in hushed tones of the reaction they'd receive back home. On our first date Kathleen took me to see *Silence Of The Lambs* and commented on how she was considering taking up her FBI offer after college. She wanted to be just like Jodie Foster in the film. I thought she was joking but she wasn't. This was only the beginning. Later in her bed she told me in a moment of self pity how she always got Lisa's offcasts and I told her we never actually slept together and she felt better then. We went at it. While we were doing it, I thought about why I never had with Lisa. Maybe it was because she thought every sexual act had to be a spiritual coming together and I didn't want to let her down. No, it was more to do with her Brontëan idea of passion. Everything had to be gothic; she once gave me a massage and nearly broke my shoulder. Kissing you she'd nearly take your mouth off. It was like being in bed with a hurricane. My penis was hard for a while and then it would just go. Lisa wasn't patient or dexterous enough to get it back. She'd just keep crashing onto me. We spent a few nights together and I'd wake up the next morning looking like I'd climbed the mountains in the Tour De France. On reflection Cathy and Heathcliff never actually slept together and this probably fitted Lisa's English fantasy.

Kathleen slowly tried to God Squad me. She'd leave little leaflets in the flat. She had all these black women round for meetings. I'd come in pissed, take the piss. They pitied me, tried to divert me from the path of evil. Fuck this, I said, I'm going back out again. It's funny how you can not like a woman and keep going back for more. There was something about her religiosity which turned me on. You want Jesus to save you, I thought, here, take him between your legs.

Too Much Like Me Girl

This isn't just prevalent in men. A woman I saw briefly at college told me she felt similar. She'd lost her first love. Was hurt badly. Her broken heart had never repaired. Now she just couldn't feel for anyone. She just went from one man to the next. She was a stunning girl with a smile to light up any London day. She could have anyone she wanted. She invited me back to her council flat. It was on the sixteenth floor. Her bed was raised and she had no curtains. I felt like the whole of London was about to watch me try and make love to this goddess. She had Chaka Khan posters on her wall. A taste for black men. She shared her flat with three other women and an ex-boyfriend cycle courier who slept on the couch. Every man I met through her was an ex-boyfriend or so it seemed. That was probably just my paranoia. The stench from his boots/socks dominated the corridor/bath-room area. I went in there to wash my face. Try and get it together! I screamed at my reflection. I couldn't get a hard-on. I couldn't relax. I went down on her for a short period and the next day she told me she might have contracted herpes. Great! I said. It was that sort of relationship. She wouldn't let me touch her in public. Not even a kiss to say Hello! We never actually split because you never knew if you were on with her or not. Suddenly you'd get a phone call and all excited. Then she'd take you round some moronic drug dealer/club promoter friend of hers and he'd drive you round like a madman to go meet someone else and go to this place and why and I'm bored and I'm leaving…

Years later I ran into her again. She'd been involved with some guy for a long while. They'd just split but she was pleased with herself. Said they split because he'd changed or something, lost his confidence but she was happy because she thought she could never love again and she honestly felt she loved him.

Why isn't he with you then? I thought. If you're in love with someone how can you split because he's lost his confidence?! I didn't say anything, we went on to a club where a friend of mine was Deejaying and had a marginally better time than we usually would clubbing. More people to talk to.

The Suicide Case

On the phone she'd always go on about her mother, which was weird. But there lay the root of her problem. Her mother and her had this love/hate thing which never let up. This girl was pretty but in a kind of long black curly hair obvious sort of way. She looked like that girl in the Nescafé ad, you know the one who parks her car on the edge of a cliff to watch the sun rise and has that weird implement which enables her to heat her Nescafé from the car battery. You know the one. Fucking shite. Anyway Nescafé had all these razor marks on her wrists when I met her. She'd tie little scarflets round them. I wasn't sure she really liked me and I wasn't that bothered but we kept this up for a few months probably because her best friend was dating mine and wanted another couple to go out with. The first time I went down to see her I was driving pissed and skidded my car right across her front lawn to signal my arrival. There was no father in the house so I didn't move it, just left it there, the mother didn't care. It wasn't like they had a flower bed or anything. I went up to her room and it was all Laura Ashley middle-class nightmare and I did my habit of walking round the outside and picking things up and looking at them. A kind of conversation substitute.

I hate it when people do that, she said.

I didn't stop.

We went and met up with our friends and after eating got invited back to her best friend's house. On the way my mate filled me in on how much the dad hated him and how he'd actually had a fight with him last weekend after he caught his daughter midnight creeping. My mate explained that he was wearing his CND T-shirt because her father worked for British Nuclear Fuels. All right, I said, I get the picture.

We went back there and helped ourselves to beer and food from the fridge, even though we'd just been to a nightmare Pizza Hut. The women insisted on watching some brat pack film which we took the piss out of and they took seriously and then we partnered off and they went upstairs and I was left with Nescafé in the front room.

What are those marks on your wrist? I asked subtly.

She said nothing. Looked like a wounded deer.

Why did you try and kill yourself? Tell me, I'm genuinely interested.

It's none of your business.

Fair enough, I said. We'd been seeing each other a month then. I'd never slept with her. She was a virgin and if you went anywhere near her she flinched.

On our last night together we all went out as a gang to Leicester Square. We had a Chinese and then went to see a film at Empire. I don't know who chose this but it turned out to be *Extremities* with Farah Fawcett Majors. Now I don't know if you've seen this but it's a long rape-ordeal film. Some of the men we were with laughed along at some of the rapist's wisecracks. I was too bored to laugh. My mate was horrified. He wanted to leave but I'd snuck some vodka and orange in in a hip flask and kept him dossed up with it. The significant thing about this night was a good friend of theirs died in a swimming pool accident right at the moment we were leaving the cinema. Nescafé asked me if she'd said anything to me at that precise moment. Probably get your hands out of my knickers, I was thinking but stalled her. For some reason she knew the time of his death and thought it significant.

I don't know, I said, not caring. I was pissed.

Typical, she said.

Who cares anyway? I said, and immediately regretted it.

My mate who had met the man in question said he was total arsehole and we shouldn't join in this general mourning. He'd deserved to die because he was a cunt and there was already too many in the world. I'd never met him but had met enough of their male friends from the area to agree.

What did you say? She said, nearly fainting with outrage.

I said, who cares? I mumbled this but still meant it.

He was my friend, she shouted, I loved him. Do you know what that means?

Fuck off! I said, I don't need a lecture on love from a suicide case. I suppose you love him like your mother loves you?

I shouldn't have added that last bit. She slapped me round the face so hard my nose bled. I never saw her again. Six days later I heard she tried to kill herself. Did it in the bathtub this time. Her mother broke the door down, got there, just.

I've never told anyone about our last conversation. Not that I blamed myself but I didn't help.

Hit girl

Another girl I tried to see at college told me how she liked her boyfriend hitting her. They'd had some big row and he came into her bedroom and slapped her so hard across the cheek she fell to the floor.

At that moment, she explained, looking back up at him I knew I truly loved him.

I felt like vomiting in her face. But I just shrugged, walked away.

Older Women/
Young Boys 1

We were in Roald Dahl's sunhouse. We used to sneak in there as it had an exterior phone and we were into nuisance calling then. I was with my video camera friend and his younger brother. They lived just over the hedge and though we never saw the famous author everyone referred to this place as the Dahls'. While we were in there and I was ringing the Samaritans wasting their time with my act of how I was really gay and couldn't live with myself etc in walked this middle-aged woman. She was twig thin, had long brown hair and made her eyes up Cleopatra style which was currently in vogue with the Bauhaus girls at school.

What are you boys doing in here? She enquired. Her voice throaty.

Thinking on my feet as usual I carried on my gay guilt fabrication so as to gain the sympathy vote. I had to do something I felt as the previous summer we'd wrecked Dahl's garden by riding on his huge motor mower and one afternoon had hacked down an entire partition simply because I hated the sight of pre-fab. For hours and hours we smacked away at it with axes and garden tools until a neighbour came over, saw us and ran to call the police. That night the three of us were walking down to the Hop as we did every Friday and the police stopped us, asked what we had been doing that very afternoon. I stepped forward as usual. Remembering my parents had been out all day shopping, I said we were all round my house playing snooker. I gave the number if he wanted to confirm this.

Were your parents in?

No.

Not much point then is there. Okay lads? Lads, move along. Then he added in explanation, we're stopping everyone.

That's okay officer. We know what a tough job you've got.

He told us he had a description of all three vandals showed me the list of features. The woman had mismatched all the pieces. Two of us had peroxided hair and wore jeans and flying jackets. Younger brother was a skinhead then and wore a Crombie and DM's. How more simple can you get? The neighbour had said, the skinhead was blonde and little guy wore boots and and…

Anyway back in the sunhouse the middle-aged woman who'd caught us on the phone instructed me to put down the receiver and sit on the floor with her. I didn't fancy this but video maker and his younger brother did it. She got hold of younger brother and said,

If you ever think you are gay, this is how you'll know you're not.

She got a breast out then and gently forced him to touch it. She then guided his middle finger into her vagina. Video maker stared and I just stood there. Transfixed. Younger brother remembered the incident years later when I reminded him of it over a drink in The Greyhound.

Strange woman, he said smiling. Wonder what she wanted?

Was she right though. I mean did you have a stiffy? I asked.

He said nothing. He was shocked.

It was my round.

Older Women/
Young Boys 2

A similar incident which happened to me did so on a train. I was travelling with a friend back from some gig, The Jam at Ally Pally I think, when a middle-aged woman came and sat with us in first class. She was kind of glamorous in an alcoholic sort of way, her breath smelt of the stuff, but the perfume she wore was nice, and she was in furs and immaculately turned out. My friend and I were pissed in that adolescent didn't-really-finish-our-can-but-pretended-that-we-had kind of way and didn't object to her sitting with us. The journey from Waterloo to Walton On Thames takes a clean half-hour and for the length of the journey she coated off her husband and passed a flask of whisky round.

We smiled along with tales of how shit marriage was even though neither of us were from broken homes and then suddenly she turned to me and asked if I wanted to come back to her house in Guildford.

No, I said, we're getting picked up from the station.

This was a bit lame but it was all I could think of.

My parents would never have done that for me, she continued, my husband won't even do it now, expects me to get a cab.

She then went into a well rehearsed monologue about her terrible childhood, and how she always got what she wanted and how she wanted a horse and got one but what she really wanted… blah, blah, blah.

Then the whisky ran out.

Why don't you come back, she asked after seeing our disappointment at the flask being dry, there's plenty more at my place. My husband always keeps a well stocked cellar.

(I bet he does, I thought.) I can't come back with him there, can I? It was stupid of me to say this.

She pounced.

He won't care, she said, he'll be in bed. Drunk. Most probably.

I said nothing more. My friend looked at me and we were about to change carriages when she threw herself on me and stuck her tongue in my mouth. Her breath was middle-aged, whisky fouled.

I pushed her off.

Sorry lady, this is our stop.

Thankfully it was.

Groupie 1

I've been in a couple of bands over the years and we all know of lead singer appeal and its all-pervasive effect on certain women. You come off stage and don't really have to try. Couple of times it happened to me in the same venue. The King's Head, Fulham. We used to play, walk off, approach the bar and they'd approach you. Simple as that. Or they'd hang on the edge of the band crowd and stare: eventually you spoke and put them out of their misery. One night I picked up a cute chunky girl with a huge nose ring. I had to be careful kissing her as it would dig up into her. Could only kiss passionately on one side. She was pretty drunk and I caught up with her quick enough. I only drank one or two before performing, anymore and you're selling yourself/your audience short. They'd paid to get in after all and if I had any work ethic it all came out on stage. Put on a good show or put off. We chatted about the show awhile. She said how professional I seemed. Thanks I said. I was invited to a party later at some theatre people's flat I knew. None of the band were happy in that crowd and so I asked the groupie if she wanted to come along. I wasn't going to go by myself. Before leaving with me she went into this whole bizarre thing of trying to persuade her friends to come. But none of them wanted to be gooseberries so she eventually relented so long as I kissed her first, before we went outside.

That way I know you won't rape me once we leave the pub, she said.

Whatever, I said, and kissed her on the mouth, not a snog,

I wasn't keen on showing massive affection in public but enough to convince her I wasn't going to rape her, whatever that means. I mean, if she really considered that I might why did she want to come? I saw this kind of nineties paranoia as charming and warmed to her. After I had kissed her and she went to fetch her coat, one of the group of guys who followed the band but had never had the balls to come up to me and talk before sidled up in his greatcoat and said,

You're not leaving with her are you? I'll lose all respect for you if you leave with her.

Instead of telling him to fuck off, I had future bands' receipts to consider, he always came in a pack of five and we needed every punter, so I settled for saying,

If you've got any respect for me in this band you're an arsehole anyway.

He liked this. Went running off to tell his friends of my outrageousness. That's it, Slim, I said to myself, keep fanning the Manti myth.

Groupie came back and waiting for the tube I needed a piss and as there was no bog I walked to the end of the platform and went between two fences.

I thought you were going to leave me, she said.

I turned on her.

Cut out this low self esteem crap will ya! Get confident.

We kissed some more and I got to feel her up a bit until the tube came. We had to change at Earls Court and there we realised we'd left it too late to get to London Bridge and the party.

You can come back to my place if you want, she said.

Sure.

We exited to try and hail a cab. Now it was her turn to take a piss. I had to show her how to crouch without wetting herself but she still insisted I watch the road not her. I was going to tell her it turned me on to watch a woman piss and then stick my cock up her later but thought better of it. We went halves on the cab even though she lived fucking miles away, somewhere out on the North Circular. In the cab I knew I wasn't going to get laid because she said after her piss she felt sick and her stomach was hurting.

Okay, I said, wishing I'd stuck to my original plan and got a cab to London Bridge.

She lived in a five-bedroom house but thankfully everyone had gone to bed by the time we got there. In the kitchen with the toast and coffee she complained about her stomach again.

All right, all right, I said, I'll sleep on the couch.

Then she got all upset and held her stomach and I apologised and claimed I misunderstood her. She calmed down then and we went up to her bedroom. She had shaved pubes so I went down on her awhile until I realised the groans I was getting weren't from pleasure but from her stomach. I stopped.

Do you want me to get you an aspirin or something?

Just hold and kiss me will you? I'm sorry. I'm sorry. I like you honestly I just don't feel up to it. I don't want you to get the wrong idea.

Forget it. It doesn't matter.

I tried kissing her then but her nose ring kept going up into her and so I stopped. It was awkward kissing her the other way as my old neck crick came back to haunt me. Fuck this, I thought and went to sleep. I woke to the nightmare of dealing with all her housemates in the morning. All women. Half of them Antipodean. We had breakfast together and for once the sound of Capital Radio was a relief. It drowned out my pathetic attempts to wind them up. We went through the ritual number swapping gag and I pecked her on the cheek and braced myself to face the elements. The door closed behind me and I followed her instructions to the bus stop. I stood there for half an hour until a black woman plus shopping helped to break up the monotony of the last fifteen minutes.

Nice day innit? She said chuckling.

I tried to smile but I'm sure it came out as a grimace.

The bitter, cold wind of North London blew the bus ever so slowly up the hill.

Groupie 2

I'm in management, she said handing me a card, my business partner and I are opening a club in Denmark. We'd like your band to open it for us. Everything will be paid up front. You've got just the right image we've been looking for.

All right, all right, I said, let me get a drink.

She got them in. The arsehole who commented on my last groupie gave me a little wink this time. Cuntfucker approved of her. Little did he know what was to follow. Yeah she looked like a brunette Supermodel, a skinny Cindy Crawford, but…

Anyway for about an hour I sat while she got the drinks in and listened to her plans for me. I sloped off for a second to say goodbye to some good friends who had come down and when I came back she nearly had a fit.

How can you be so rude? She demanded, how can you walk off like that, just because I've gone to the bathroom, you use that as an excuse to go and speak to someone else. How dare you? No-one does that to me.

Listen lady, I retorted, this is a business night get it? If people come see me I have to go and thank them all right? Otherwise they don't come again. You of all people should know that. Now get off my case or fuck off, okay?

She was a little taken aback then.

No-one's ever spoken to me like that before. Do you know what opportunities I'm offering you? I can't believe my ears. Did you really tell me to fuck off?

Yeah, well I'm the real thing lady.

Anyway she paid for a cab back to her pad in Liverpool Street. It was all modern, black facia etc. She cut up some coke and we snorted it. I poured out some brandy. She told me what it was and how much it cost but that kind of information goes in one ear and out the other with me.

I never met anyone quite like you, she said, staring at the holes in my Converse.

Of course you haven't, I said, that's why you're going to make so much money off me.

Yes, aren't I, she said and laughed in a kind of Vaudeville Cruella De Ville manner. It didn't endear her to me.

In the sack she had one strange foible and that was to keep her breasts covered. I wasn't to touch the straps on her slip.

Fine, I said, whatever. I hitched the slip up, no knickers. Good. After we'd finished, she lit up a cigarette and then burst into tears.

This is my first one night stand ever, she sobbed.

And for the first time that night I believed her.

My husband and I had such plans, she said, such plans.

Your what? I repeated.

I was married, she said. Married, married, married.

What happened? I asked.

He killed himself six months ago.

I tried not to say WHAT? But my mouth made the shape. Jesus Christ what had I got myself into here? Some mad Danish bitch who'd only slept with her husband and then me, according to this latest little speech she's giving me and me what am I supposed to say, how can I possibly handle this?

That's sad, I said in the end. I didn't know what else to say.

The next morning she got out an ungodly amount of cash from her bank and paid for my cab back to Waterloo. She gave me her card but I never called it. I figured if she was serious about the band she could easily come along to another gig, we were in *Time Out* and *NME* every time we played. She never came. Guess she got what she wanted in the same way I had.

Ferry Crossing

I was already meeting a woman in Paris.
I didn't need to meet another on the ferry going over. She had that whimsical sixties hippie girl look, all long hair and no make up but with nineties updates like a pierced eyebrow, black leggings and DM's. She was sat behind me on the coach. Thankfully the three American girls sitting around me chatted amongst themselves briefly then shut up and slept. I could never allow myself to sleep on a coach as the askance position the head is forced into could put my neck out for weeks. The woman I was meeting in Paris liked to have sex in any number of strenuous positions and I not wanting to disappoint her – she came all the way from Spain twice a year for this – kept my gaze *toute droite*. The girl was near the back, Walkman on. I don't know whether she looked at me as I got on, baseball cap down and bandana wrapped round the neck even though it was summer (I'd heard that draughts on the neck were bad also) but if she didn't look, she certainly did on the ferry. I noticed her checking me out as we were all lined up as foot passengers at Dover.

After eating I headed to the bar and downed a couple of stiff Scotch's. She was by the window. I sat near enough for her to see it as a sign. She could act on it if she wanted to. She did. Invited me over. She was French. She asked me if I was in this club she was at last night. I knew the club, a gay club in the heart of London, but didn't see any point in lying and answered with a denial. It's strange, she said, you look just like this guy I saw. I was going to tell her that if she was going to make up something like this in future, it was better not to choose a gay club, but I'd got a good vibe off her already and so held back my natural impulse. She declined a drink, claiming the pubs in London had worn her out. I laughed. She asked where I was going. Paris, I said, you? Amsterdam. She asked me what I was doing in Paris and I made up some story about a record company meeting. Which one? She asked. Columbia, I said. Whereabouts? She asked. Near the Bastille, I invented (clever huh?) I guess I don't have to spell out why I began the lie, and as usually happens in these instances, another follows on to back up the first and so it goes... I wasn't worried though. I was a past master at keeping track.

She asked me whether I could speak French. *Petit peu*, I said. The old student standby. She then insisted we speak French for the rest of the crossing which didn't enthrall me much but I knew enough conversational gambits to get by. I also thought it might help keep my lying down to a minimum. We spoke. She told me her name but I can't remember it, Ratchel? She was from Montpellier – not a million miles from where I went to school as a boy – so we reminisced about the South a while. I smoked one of her cigarettes. I don't actually smoke but there's something about women smoking that I can't say no to. She told me about aupairing in Hampstead and I could imagine the nightmare she'd been through. Three kids, both parents out all day. Golf every weekend plus various functions, committees in the evenings. The stay had put her off work for life and I fully encouraged that sentiment, never having had a proper job in my life.

She was interested in the band and as this did actually exist although we weren't signed to Columbia, nobody in fact, I span out a few stories of gigs, studios etc. Why do people find this stuff interesting? Maybe she didn't. Maybe she just liked me. I liked her now. A lot. I wanted to kiss her. I went to the bar to get another drink, work up the courage. I also thought by demonstrating the rock 'n' roll lifestyle to her

I'd become better at embellishing it (to myself?). I'd been describing it in my stuttering French, she filling in the gaps, correcting the tenses. I figured her age to be around nineteen. Apparently she had liked kids as a kid and so just fell into aupairing. She was a natural. *Comme Princess Di*? I offered and she laughed. Like a lot of European hippies she wore one of those Duran Duran scarves which went out of fashion almost as soon as they came in in the mid-eighties. It didn't matter though, the English will always forgive the slightly backward nature of Europe on this front. Why? They forgive us nothing.

I told her the record company wanted me to fly out but I couldn't stand aeroplanes. She told me I was crazy, anybody choosing to travel by coach and ferry needed their head tested (I forget the French for this). She then asked me why I didn't take the Eurostar and I had to make up another lie about no bookings. We went out onto the deck and I studied her profile while she looked out. Another ferry passed. The moment passed when I could have kissed her. The Tannoy announcement broke my nerve and we followed the others, making our way to the stairs. She waited for me as I went into the washroom and coming out she was standing there... This was it, I thought, if you want to kiss her do it now. Did I want to? Yes. Did I kiss her? No. It was somehow better that way.

I'd given her my phone number in London but I knew she'd never call. She was going to Amsterdam to start a new life for herself. She had no forwarding address. She got on another coach and I stood there for one mad second and considered joining her. Why was I going to Paris? I didn't love the woman there. It was just sex. But what was this? Love? It felt like it as I passed her window and she looked out at me, smiling. The pain I experienced dragging myself back to my seat and watching her coach pull off! Her face was pressed to the glass all the way, all the way, all the way...

Maybe I should have followed her? But how? I didn't even know her surname. I'd told her a pack of lies. Not the best way to start a relationship. Maybe we'd had the perfect time on that ferry… Amsterdam didn't interest me. Paris didn't particularly interest me either but the woman's body I was meeting there did. I didn't mention the ferry crossing or the girl to her. We met outside the Louvre, went for a beer, headed for the hotel.

The Chicken Korma Story

I'd been seeing this woman for a while and had put a lot of work into our relationship. I really liked her. But there was one problem blocking us, and in the end it proved insurmountable. Her ex-boyfriend. Nothing unusual there I know, except she still lived in the same house as him. Had her own room you understand and a studio he'd built for her and now I think you can begin to appreciate my apprehension when she first invited me back. I guess part of it was my fault because I didn't have my own place at the time. I was living back at home while I paid off some debts and so wasn't in any position to advise her to move, if you see what I mean. I met her in the pub I drank in, I was sitting there proofreading a friend's poetry manuscript when she came over and asked what I was studying. I'd noticed her before, of course, but as she always seemed to be with a bunch of people and I was usually on my own I didn't rate my chances. Anyway I was only there to get out of the house. She liked the poetry so much she even jotted down some lines in her notebook. I thought this a little rude but didn't want to blow my chances by reminding her of copyright or whatever and in any case I shouldn't have worried because then she sat with me and I told her of my work and she had family in publishing and was only too willing to share her contacts. I got her address and sent her the two books. Then we began to meet up more regularly but Alfred was always there. Yes, the ex-boyfriend. He'd made a million inventing some time-delay contraption on burglar alarms. He tried to explain it to me over and over but all I could think of was, What's the point of a time delay on a burglar alarm?

I'm sure there was some reason but I was there to hear what she had to say anyway. This set the pattern for the few months we were together. He called me an unpleasant boy once and I nearly hit him out on the footpath until he said, I detest all violence. And as I liked that line I warmed to him but only for about half a second. I couldn't see what this talented painter with publishing contacts was doing with this silly businessman. That's the only word I can use to describe him, silly. Of course he probably wasn't but I was just so jealous I couldn't see further than the end of her nose. Ah, but what a nose, aquiline, expressive!

I had to admit the first time I saw the house I was impressed. Backed up on the Thames and she had her own veranda where we sat and watched the boats. Her studio had a pine floor and an endless supply of expensive materials. All on Alfred's account, I gathered. The fact that I loved her work made it all the worse of course. We couldn't go out for a Friday night drinking session without him coming along. I warned her that I get nasty when I drink and she said, Nonsense you're such a good writer, how can you let yourself be dragged down by such vulgarity? A good question. You'll get used to him, she said, don't forget I still love him as a friend and it's important to me that you grow to love him as well. I don't care how long it takes. Maybe she was right but I wasn't famous for my patience mainly because I'd been so patient for fame I had none left for my personal life. I just fucking hated him and it was so childish because he was so much older than me and so different, why couldn't I accept him? Not that he was any more mature about me.

Anyway cut to the chicken. I managed to have one Friday night alone with her in the pub and we came back well pissed and Alfred had gone to bed.

Is it all right if I help myself to some food? I asked in all innocence. I'd done it many times before with no comeback.

Sure, she said, I'm going to take a shower, okay?

This wasn't unusual for she usually came to the pub paint-splattered right after working and I sat with her and scraped the colours from her strong hands with my nails.

Seeing a large pot of chicken that no-one had eaten, I dug in.

The next morning Alfred broke the one rule he'd kept so far and came into her bedroom and shook us awake.

Alfred, she exclaimed, Alfred what is it?

Who's eaten the chicken korma?! He shrieked. He looked as if he was going to have a cardiac there and then.

The what? She said.

The chicken korma! The curry I'd been cooking for my parents all evening while you were down the pub, which is where I wanted to be but no, my dear mother and father are coming up today, in case you've forgotten, which you obviously have with lover boy here, now I don't care about him, this isn't about him, unless...

He looked right at me.

He ate the chicken korma!

Don't call me lover boy, I said.

Just answer the fucking question!!

I asked first, I said, thinking I would have lied if I didn't care so much about her. Didn't I? I turned to her, I asked first.

She said nothing and he used her silence as tacit agreement and launched into a speech of everything he didn't like about me which I'll spare you.

I wasn't scared of him and refused to put my clothes on as he instructed unless she told me to go. She didn't exactly but then she tried to make out that when she said help yourself she didn't mean the dish with tin foil over but she'd never made that distinction the night before and we both knew, so I left. I let Alfred have his hollow triumph not because I cared about him, I was just disappointed at her weakness.

Stick your chicken korma up your arse! I shouted, slamming the door, a typically pointless parting shot.

Walking away, now I actually like this guy! I thought.

Now I'd seen the passion he had. That's what she loved in him. Fucking hell another thing to be jealous of! I slapped my forehead. Maybe they were better off together. I wished them well.

.

Scarf Story

Big B prized his cashmere scarf like a china doll. Once when we were larking about at a station he span round and it fell out of his pocket. Without him noticing I kicked the scarf underneath the seat and then slid it into my pocket as we got on the train. Sitting down I'm waiting for the train to just pick up enough speed so he won't be able to jump out…

'Isn't that your scarf on the station there? There, look on the bench.'

He checks his pockets. Jumps up.

'Fuck. That's my cashmere,' he's going, 'that's a family heirloom. My gran gave me that before she died. It was her scarf. My fucking family cashmere!'

I sit down, poker-faced but cracking inside. He hasn't even looked back at the platform, which if he had, he would realise it was way too gloomy for me to just be able to spot it in the half-light! Honestly the way I got up and looked! He hasn't even noticed my hands stuffed into my Harrington to disguise the bulge.

His scarf! His cashmere!

How he used to Lord it over us, the fucker, I decide to prolong the agony. Near the next station, he announces he's going to get out, change sides and get the first train back.

'It'll still be there,' I reassure, letting an ounce of doubt creep into my voice.

'It better be,' he says, 'otherwise I'm dead. My dad's gonna kill me.'

I let him off then. Threw the scarf in his face.

'You bastard!' He spat. But he knew. A little spark of admiration flashed from his eyes.

Bully

In winter I devised a way of crucifying people with scarves. One round the feet, two round the wrists. It was easier to hang people upside down we found, reverse stigmata, then you could get three up on the playground fence before a teacher came. Again my so-called humiliations backfired, people began to volunteer to be crucified. They gained a kind of weird cult status from being done.

Head bully was a Greek guy who seemingly had it all. Charm, model good looks, strength and a bullying mind that can only be described as ingenious. He invented the classic Collarado. Noting that once the collars of school shirts were marked with black indelible pens they didn't wash out, and that the exercise could be done in class, without the victim sitting in front knowing, the quick swipe across the back of the shirt quickly caught on. To be Collaradoed was a serious face-loss. There was even a school assembly to discuss the ongoing Collarado crisis. One mother had complained that all five of little Johnnie's school whites had been Collaradoed and could the Head see to it that the instigators were punished and some compensation meted out. To be cool was to sit at the back of the class, of course, pen in hand, and have pristine whites.

Trying to outdo the Greek guy became a school obsession and when the Superglue phase started, many believe he was surpassed. Personally I didn't think gluing a fourteen-year-old girl to a toilet seat so that she had to be carried out to the ambulance, sheet over, still sitting on the seat, to be an advancement. Sure, as pure theatre it was gothic in its hilarity, but little Johnnie's shirts fade eventually, imagine Missy coming back to school the next day, physically unharmed maybe but psychologically...

The thing to remember was 'bonds in seconds.' The one time it nearly happened to me, reaching for a cup of tea after I turned back from talking to someone, I felt that initial rush as the glue tried to stick, but just managed to stretch skin away from crockery before the two met permanently. Then you had to stay calm and not even touch your fingers together before reaching the bathroom. Taking the towel carefully in your other hand you wipe quickly so that the material doesn't stick also. My older brother was not as lucky, but he said it was painless at the hospital and over in seconds.

BMX

We'd get the second-years to lie on their backs, five in a row, launch up the ramp and jump them on the BMX. This became another great spectacle and in my enthusiasm for grand theatre, I as ringmaster wanted to go one better. Instead of having five second-years to jump; I wanted six. No-one wanted to be the sixth, of course, muggins on the end. I had to march round and force someone. This kid was clever though; really didn't want to do it. He'd seen the last three jumps just clear five. But I wasn't having any of his objections and after he joined the row and got up, bottling for the second time, I went over and forced him to lie on the ground. He wasn't having it though, and as he came up, crying and pleading, I rammed my knee into his nose. Blood was everywhere, somebody screamed. Then everyone scarpered as the Head Teacher came out. Now then, here was a situation. I was already on report, which meant getting a form signed at the end of every class to say how I'd behaved etc and then presenting it at the end of every day to my form teacher for her to sign so I could get out of school and get home. And one more piece of trouble this term would have meant a suspension. The second-year in question, who'd cleaned himself up now, just a bleed it wasn't broken, sat next to me. We were out in the corridor, by the Head Teacher's office. I had to work quickly.

Look, sorry about the nose, just got a bit carried away. You know with the BMX and everything, you know, the way everyone loves it?

He nodded at this, slightly. Tried to wipe his face as if it was sweat and dirt he was dealing with, not the residue of tears.

And if I get done for this, I explained, I'll be expelled. I'm already on report.

Really, he said. Impressed. Being on report was cool. It meant your parents knew, as they had to sign the form too.

I'm really sorry about your nose, as I said it was just enthusiasm okay? Now if you tell her exactly what happened, I'll be expelled, you don't want that do you?

No, but. . It's out of my hands. I told her it was you.

Told her what though?

That you forced me to stand up and kneed me in the face.

Right! Forced you to stand up, you didn't mention the BMX or the line-up or you watching, or me forcing you to lie down did you?

No.

Okay. Here's the deal. You won't get touched ever again for your whole school life, in fact you'll get privileges; if you just say you weren't sure.

How do you mean?

I'm not asking you to deny it was me. Just say you weren't sure.

Will that be enough?

Trust me.

So anyway we get in there and the Head Teacher asks me to explain my actions of course, and what the commotion around the bike sheds was about. I explain how, in my maturity, I could see the potential danger of using human beings like circus animals and went over there to break up the BMX show.

You were trying to break it up? She asks, astonished.

Yes. It was when I was dragging Rufus here away from danger that the unfortunate accident occurred.

So you're not denying the act took place?

I'm denying it was deliberate. I was breaking it up.

Rufus?

I'm not sure. Miss.

But you told me earlier it was Slim here who attacked you.

I, uh… I can't be sure.

And that was it. Rufus got a week of detentions for being involved and I was exonerated. Even got a nod of gratitude and taken off report a week later for my 'in-time attitude.'

Wrecking Crew

We'd saunter into the kitchen, pretend to know a few people, sneak some beer when no-one was looking then Jay headed to the front room and changed the tape. I'd go upstairs with Grace, and she'd begin to undress on the bed while I ransacked the drawers for clothes, money, jewellery. Anything we couldn't stuff into trouser pockets we chucked out the window, onto the drive, by the getaway car. Ghetto blasters, golf clubs, weights, anything. Grace would undress in case the host walked in and found us in his room. He'd know what we were up to then. One time this actually did occur, the light came on and there I was, stuffing a top down my trousers.

Hey what are you doing in here?

What do you think we're doing?

This is my bedroom.

Sorry man the door was open.

Well you'll have to leave.

Fine. We didn't think it was an uptight scenario.

Sorry?

Uptight, you know, no sex.

And who the fuck are you?

Well I'm me, aren't I. And you're you.

Slim… (this was Grace, on the bed)

All right. Look we just wanted somewhere private I didn't know it was your room man, come on, we'll leave, it's cool.

He was about to accept that when he saw the open drawers.

Why are these drawers open?

Dunno, I said, we've just come in here.

But why are these open? And what's that bulge in your pocket? I saw you stuffing something down there.

What do you think it is? Are you insulting my woman?

We opened the drawers to look for protection.

Again this was Grace. Another stroke of inspiration. He just about accepted that. We finished dressing and left. Nothing missing anyway. Shit stuff in the drawers, only crappy Jockey Y-Fronts and jumpers. I rearranged the bulge so it went down my trouser leg and we walked down, gave the leaving nod to the others and exited. Thought it was a Smedley top I'd nicked but it was only lambswool so I threw it out the window as we drove away. Fuck it, I said, that was close.

The Wrecking Crew consisted of Grace and I, Jay the skiing instructor from Sandown Park (strictly matted slopes), Gino the nervous Italian and Henry the driver, our back-up. He liked to fight. Enjoyed rolling people around when he was winning, banging their heads on the concrete. He was there to bail us out, drive.

A guy I worked with, marking up the morning papers, was a new arrival to the area and eager to make friends. Throw a party I suggested. Good idea, he says, my parents are away in South Africa at the moment, what about Saturday night? Perfect. But I'm worried about turn-out, he said, can you invite everyone you know? Sure I said. Don't you worry about it. I'll get a good crowd down there. The house was in Durwood Park, had its own tennis court, underground disco, the whole bit. I was on the door. Don't know how it got started really, this wasn't a Wrecking Crew exercise, although they were there. At some point the whole house was stripped. Someone started clowning around with some garden furniture out back; soon enough that went in the pool. I was asked by the host to inspect one of the bedrooms which had been covered in felt tip graffiti and the bed was wet with piss. I was amused/annoyed that some of the graffiti was about me. I shrugged my shoulders. Fuck knows. Well I didn't do it did I? I'm not going to write graffiti about myself am I? Give me a few years maybe, but not now. Because I was away from the door some of Walton's worst were let in, and soon enough people were walking out with records, stereos, the television. Jay was swinging from the chandeliers and our host came over and shouted: Control them! Nothing to do with me, I stated, Call the police, that way everyone will leave. But I can't, he says, then my parents will find out. Fair enough I said, it will die down. Anyway by the end of the night ten thousand pounds worth of damage was done. He told me about it at work Monday morning. He tried to get a list of names out of me but I wasn't buying. I mean you do a lot of things but you don't grass.

When the Wrecking Crew no longer began to hear about parties we changed our focus to wedding receptions and clubs. The wedding thing was my idea. There was nothing I liked more than smash and grab and what better way to spend a weekend than driving around churches and country hotels gate-crashing receptions? In we walked, bold as brass, and not even bothering to change so we could at least mingle. There they all were, top hats and tails, dresses and veils and we were still in jeans and Converse, flying or skiing jackets, our hair Brylcreamed, the others kind of rockabilly, Gino and I still Mods. We'd bowl straight over and help ourselves to champagne, the buffet before a couple of the men came over and ejected us; none too gently most times, I can tell you. Anyway, that got boring after a few black eyes and we had to drag Henry away once after the best man punched him in the Adam's Apple. It went straight up the back of his throat and his face turned purple. He lay on the ground, screaming, choking, rolling around. 'Help me! Help me!' He gurgled. And for once, we did.

Dingwall's was the club we went to. Henry liked to wind up the Hell's Angels down there. We danced thrash style then, everyone did. Clear your little space on the dance floor. Then he drove us back pissed down the A3, all the way home.

Drink and driving was about then but it was kind of like it is in France now, if you don't wreck anything/one you won't get done. We were a typical gang, anyone outside of it was dismissed.

A typical example of my attitude was a party I attended with Grace. The host kept trying to chat us up, get us in with his crowd.

Are you two locals? He asked finally, across the room loudly.

I waited for the silence to settle before replying,

I live in London actually, I share a flat with the Right Honourable Okey Wambeyzee, African Warrior.

Of course there was nothing anyone could say to that. I remember the look of incredulity which overcame my questioner. Grace just laughed. That's what we had really. She laughed at everything I said. Wouldn't it be horrible to be ugly? She said, looking over at their table. I'd hate to be ugly. She wasn't, but to me, she never looked as beautiful again.

The Wrecking Crew split when my mum's car got smashed. Another night driving up to Dingwall's, all of us pissed, a bottle of whisky going round, my Mini broken down and me stupidly borrowing my mum's new Renault Five and getting too drunk to drive. Henry driving as usual. I had no worries there. He was the best out of all of us; he'd even done that police advanced drivers' course for some reason. I think his old man was a judge or something, set it up for him as a birthday treat. Old Henry spinning those double deckers around, handbrake-turning panda cars. So there we were jumping lights, rocking the car, cutting people up. In London the police do pull you over, and they did, maybe for overloading, I don't know, perhaps Henry jumped a red light, who knows? He goes to reverse and park when suddenly he slams it in first and away we go, the policeman hitting his hand on top of the car as we just miss him, swerve and head towards Kentish Town.

Stunned, I'm going; Henry what are you doing? Why didn't you stop?

Why do you think? They'd throw the fucking book at us. Don't worry, I've done this before. You just sit tight. We'll be on the motorway in no time.

And he had done it before. I'd never been party to one of these trips, but it was what had made his name. Henry the Driver. Escapologist. Better driver than the Law. Had never crashed a car in his life. And though I was sitting there shitting myself and pleading with him not to crash, to stop, get out and run and I'd say I was driving, say he kidnapped the car, anything, just as long as the car was all right. Meanwhile us switch-backing all through North London and as yet we've only got the one copper on our tail and he's losing us. Henry is driving like a man inspired, we take corners on two wheels, go through council estates as I sit there praying no kid steps from the kerb at the wrong moment. Miraculously we hit nothing, no parked cars, lamposts, nothing. Henry seems to know his way and all the time he's planning the next move. Right here, left here, u-ey here. And chill Slim, don't worry, you're the only one they're going to be able to trace, through your mum's registration, so listen, as soon as we get on the motorway then it's home with the car and we'll dump it in Esher Woods. Get home, get up and say the car's been stolen. Let the police find it and we're sorted.

This sounded like a mad plan to me, but I could see it could work and Jay the ski instructor assures me they've done it before and even though the police know, there's nothing they can do.

Right, right I'm going. Just don't crash the car. I'm going.

And I know he won't. You really have to experience the strange ease of a police chase with a top driver in command. I just knew they weren't going to catch us. Sure we had one copper on our tail, and he was probably on the radio to the SPG, but these were the days before infra-red helicopters capturing you for Crime Monthly and even though we weren't losing the policeman, he wasn't catching us and soon we'd be on the motorway...

We never got to the motorway.

It wasn't Henry's driving that let him down but his knowledge. Somehow we ended up in a building site, he skidded the car to a halt, handed me the keys and instructed everyone to scale the fence. At that moment the police car came crashing into the driver's door-buckling it so Henry couldn't get out. The others panicked, jumped out and Henry grabbed the keys back saying,

It doesn't matter now, it's damaged! And began to reverse. As he backed up he didn't realise one of the doors was open and so he totalled that on the brick wall behind. By now the copper was getting out of his car, holding his head from smacking it on the dashboard in the act of ramming us, and Henry could see there was no way he could reverse out of the angle he'd trapped us in. We both climbed out and he ran for it. I just stood there. In despair at my mum's car. I wasn't worried about the policeman, the others. It was just that phone call I was worried about, and all this getting out.

Henry got fined thousands and they tried to pin an assault charge on him when the copper hit his hand on the roof of the car as we pulled off but the judge was having none of it.

I had to work a night-shift factory job to pay off the five hundred pounds for two new doors and that was end of the Wrecking Crew. Payback.

Hotel

Somehow the Irish lad acquired a key to the bell tower. From there you could get up on to the slate roof and edge your way into any open window. We found out what time dinner was served and planned our raids around then. Hotel rooms are surreal in their uniformity. Again it was in and out, the kind of job I liked most. The same old hoard: clothes, wallets, jewellery, and a portable TV if we felt adventurous. There was no buzz like entering the room though, searching round with torches, opening and closing drawers. We were careful in that we made sure the occupants were leaving for the evening before entering. Sometimes we crouched on those roofs for hours; all blacked up waiting for the light to go.

Golf Club

This establishment was so exclusive and up its own arse all the members left their clubs in a coveted shed shaded by trees. It wasn't even in sight of the pro's shop! To get the key was my job. Confidence trick again. Put on a plummy voice, get all dressed up, pay for a round on the short course (five pounds, a fortune for us but a sound investment as it turned out). Say Daddy's a member, give out a name you've overheard in the members' bar, they write it in the log book and then hand over the key to the members' shed so you can borrow his clubs. Say you got lost, went to the wrong shed before handing it back; time enough for your mate to cycle down the hill to the High Street, get the key cut and back. Back again at the dead of night, and remember on bloody pushbikes for Christ's sake! Grab two bags and cycle to the Scout Hut. We put them, fence side, underneath in a little pit where the firing corps used to leave their expended magazines and not even the Scouts stored anything and then bold as you like put an ad in the local rag the week after. We sold the hugely expensive clubs for a knockdown rate, businessmen so happy they'd found a couple of mugs who'd had clubs left to them in a will.

Village Hall

Christmas was always a good money spinner. Nicking bottles of Grolsch from Zelda's wine bar we heard this noise… The Village Hall's back window flapping. A bit of prying, a quick leg up, and we were in. Not fathoming that here the Post Office used the space for their annual over-spill of parcels we landed in a veritable Aladdin's cave of pressies. We checked the name tags with our torches and filled our Christmas lists with other people's presents. Then we allowed ourselves a general rampage through some of the more interesting parcels. Remember, we only took what we could carry in our rucksacks as we had to climb back out again to go undetected. We were never caught because we kept to these rules. Always clear up after yourselves; I've never understood why burglars leave a mess. We were locals after all. We didn't want an investigation. We wanted to come back next year. We took all the brown paper with us and had a little bonfire over the park, comparing finds. Anything crap we didn't want we took with us also, we sold almost every-thing at the village annual car boot sale held after New Year's. A piquant pleasure was imagining we'd achieved the double con: members of the public buying back what conceivably could have been theirs.

Cars

It started with just going round nicking things out of them. Coats, bags, suitcases, tapes, whatever. We never got much from this until we started knocking about with a Bedfont casual who showed us how to nick any old Ford model with a sharpened fifty-pence piece. It was roughly the key's diamond shape and you had to jimmy up the lock a bit and force it but sure enough it opened and also started a lot of the ignitions; though the Irish lad had learned to hot wire then which I never did. The system was again late night, jimmy the lock and roll the car out of the parking space/garage. It always had to be on a hill; that way you could jump in and roll before starting. Most people know the sound of their own cars firing in the driveway, but down the road it could be anyone's. No-one ever came out. We used to take the cars up to parties and pubs and drive them round London, often returning them to a neutral place where we could all walk home from, but essentially undamaged. Sometimes we returned them to the same street. We weren't joyriders in the sense of taking on the police, smashing things up.

Politics

We were thrown out the Walton Labour Party for picketing the local station for allowing night trains of nuclear waste through. They saw us as radicals. They needed to merge with the Liberals to get any votes.

Black Culture

There was only one at the comprehensive I went to, but I soon took him under my wing. Why I did this, I don't know. I saw him all alone, it didn't matter whether I liked him or if we had anything in common; I gave him specialist treatment, let him hang out with my crew. Reverse racism, I suppose you could call it. Reggae was all we listened to. David Rodigan, every Saturday night. Eight o'clock sharp. Capital Radio. Giles Peterson down the Belvedere in Richmond, Sunday night. Ideas from jazz scribbled on scraps of paper like, 'the world is round but thinks square.' When Rap came in with Run DMC and the Beasties, calling your women 'bitch' became cool for a while, difficult to explain this one. A friend says he still finds himself slipping into it occasionally, now of course he's doing it deliberately, ironically, as if somehow he's not testing her reaction to sexism, some power struggle, but in fact seeing how down she is; seeing if she's down with the homeboys. What cack. Yo! We'd all go.

Sunday Lunch

I'd sit there and tell stories about drug dealer friends who'd had human fingers sent to them in the post. Warnings not to splice amounts. Don't put your fingers in my stash in other words. And then go into a whole monologue about how so-and-so has a house already and a car and all because he pays students safe-house money so he's never got anything at his place. And he never sells to anyone over anything but a mobile, and anyone dodgy he says no to.

Of course I'm not involved in any of it, I just feel as Samantha's boyfriend it's my role to keep you informed.

Skid in the gravel drive arriving and leaving.

Taking the Piss

Big B had the brainwave of translating the term literally. Halfway through he got a bit bored with the wall and aimed at the empty glass. Filling it, he brought it back into the car, much to the driver's chagrin, but as Big B was bigger than him, he did what he liked. So round we span with it, until someone had the brilliant/cuntish brainwave of stopping at the first lone homewalker, pretending to ask for directions and then flinging the pint of piss in his face. We did this a few weekends running until we did it to the wrong guy and the word went out. Last time it was almost like he knew it was coming, I wound down the window, put on my professor-plum accent, asked the question, got him to bend down, come nearer, but he knew, something about the way he didn't get too close, didn't edge too far down. He grabbed the pint when I flicked my wrist and more went on me, the window, down the interior than him.

One of our crew got this fifteen-year-old pregnant and tried to pass the buck. All in the local paper it was, him going, Well I told her to have an abortion. Stupid cunt. Should have kept that to himself.

Pranks

First one was ring up a dork's girlfriend and ask to speak to her parents. Usually this dork was on the fringes of the cool crew and would do anything to get in, even telling us about dirty-fucking his girlfriend, her shouting Ram it in! Ram it in! With her folks asleep next door. Anyway we'd ring up, then when mum or dad came to the phone, we'd say hello you don't know me but I'm a friend of blah and blah and it's my understanding that your daughter's pregnant. Yes I was shocked. Well no, Blah is my best friend and he wanted to tell you with Blah but I know him, he's a shy boy you know, so I just thought it was in your interest and from a friendship point of view, you know, figured it was my responsibility to tell you.

After this came the death announcement. Ring someone's dad while you're having a drink with them somewhere or you're both at some party and speak in hushed tones of the dreadful car accident you've just witnessed outside. They come haring down, rush into the party to see their son happily drinking away, and then you sit back as all hell lets loose. A milder version was the old call someone at three in the morning, wait for fifteen or so rings for Daddy to get up and answer and then just as he says Hello? You hang up. He doesn't know who it is of course but your mate does, although he doesn't know which of his friends, and so can only retaliate by doing it back to whoever he thinks it is. And so on. It was usually a weekend night, and one of two people doing it. Gino the Italian, or one his associates. I hadn't had one for ages and for some reason felt I was next in line, just happened to be up – a late night vid sess – watching the end of *Apocalypse Now*. It rang. I jumped up, picked it up on the first ring. A shocked breath on the other end. Nothing said. Gino, I gloat, I know it's you. Don't ever fucking do it again.

Inter Rail

It wasn't cool to be in Italy just after the Heysel disaster and Gino was the only one who didn't get his change thrown back at him in cafes. We weren't from Liverpool for Christ's sake! Anyway we didn't stay there long. Took pictures of us doing moonies in the confessional boxes inside the Vatican. One of somebody sucking the teat on a statue, you know, usual juvenile stuff. Our first stops had been Amsterdam and Paris. In Amsterdam we played frisbee over everyone's tents on the campsite, hired bikes, smoked hashish and chatted up American girls at the Hard Rock Café. In Paris it was too expensive for us to do much, just got some wine in and kept everyone awake in the dorm. Left the next day for Germany where again we got in trouble for playing frisbee on some official square in Munich. From there we got a train to Dachau and larked about in the camp while everyone else adopted the solemn faces they considered appropriate. The guide told us if the Jews lost their bowl they'd starve and I went, Oh so they got to play cricket then? Gags like that.

Next stop Rome, I remember Trevor and Cornelius constantly wanting to sightsee, and me and Gino going: Enough! And just lying on these walls all day sleeping. Big B was along for the trip but that was a serious mistake on his part, as he'd more or less stopped hanging round with us prior to this and was now part of the drug crowd. Or wanting to be. We heard if there was a car full he'd be left behind so maybe that engendered his insecurity and made him come along. Big B and me were the only ones with rucksacks while the others thought it would look cooler to have shoulder-type holdalls and carry extras like tent paraphernalia separately. Big B and I stuffed all our poles in one package as this was cheaper at left luggage. The others whined and played out no end of resentment for having to pay for two or three items while we only paid for one.

Serves you right, sneered Big B, just cause you wanted to be cool and have a shoulder bag, now you're paying for it.

But you could go halves on the tent…

Oh no, we've got the poles in the tops of our bags just 'cause your pathetic little yuppie packs won't carry anything, that's not our problem.

I of course sided with Big B, gaining cool marks from an uncool accessory.

Gradually this trip turned into a cool act blueprint. Gino and I wrote up a clippable offence manifesto. Basically anything uncool was clippable. A sharp flick, inside of the hand, across the offender's crown for any of the following offences.

Stating the obvious. (I just did; explaining the clip) Repetition. Overacting. Homesickness. Cliches. Gullibility. Changing the past to suit your purpose. Lying. Gross stupidity. Physical disgustingness. Telling an unfunny joke. Singing 'Just One Cornetto' in Venice.

At any of these offences someone would pounce, stating, That is severely clippable!

Any clippable accusation could be appealed at the High Court. For this to work and the clip nullified the accused must have at least two others to overturn the accuser. Voting majority decided. Of course, losing in the High Court meant the original clip punishment was turned into a group slap. The loser had to bend his head down as we all stood in a circle and slapped our hands down as hard as we could for a few seconds. Very few High Court decisions were ever overturned as High Court Beatings proved so enjoyable. Gino took the process a stage further by conning Big B once into thinking he had his vote then changing back at the last minute. Big B tried to argue he wouldn't have taken the charge to the High Court if he didn't think he had Gino's vote, but as gullibility was already an offense he lost.

It was a miserable trip for him. All he did was make a remark to the effect that a man's opened belt strap in a park in Paris had looked like his penis from a distance. Although he was only adjusting his trousers, it appeared as if he was taking a piss. I could sort of see what he meant but the clipping process had got so vicious by this stage it was too delicious to ignore. Gino tried to argue he should also get a second clip for falling for a double con. But as it wasn't written in the manifesto we let it pass.

We took the boat from Brindisi to Greece and spent our last week there. Big B went off on his own most the time, met a girl, moved into her tent. I hung out with Gino as neither of us had the skin to sunbathe. We played a lot of chess. Trevor and Cornelius went off, happy together, likewise. On the ferry back to Athens Big B and I played frisbee on the deck and later I met an Italian girl and spent the night with her amongst the huge sea ropes at the front. Trevor and Cornelius met some Scandinavians on the train back to Paris and they followed us to London. And finally we all got to Walton station and had to spend an hour in police cells. In our home town, we got wrongly arrested for vagrancy! I mean we did look all dirty with sleeping bags over our shoulders but come on! We wanted to get home and have a bath.

Taking the Piss 2

If you're dying for a piss you can shout Relief three times at the top of your voice and relieve yourself anywhere. Of course some stupid fuckers tried it outside Woolworth's and then the police station!

DM Laces Differentiation

At the football anyone wearing DM's had to take their laces out and leave them by the toilets. This was an amazing sight. Row upon row of different coloured laces, hundreds of them, all hung out as if some lace company were using the terraces as drying racks. DM laces had colour/power differentiation also. Black for regular geezers. Red if you were cool, imaginative but still not really up for it (me). Blue if you were Chelsea crew and counted and accepted (made your bones in other words). White if you were rock hard. Skins and psychos wore white laces. You can see them coming on a dark night. I only wore DMs for about a year though, then mostly trainers. Bjorn Borg Gold Adidas, Gazelles, Filas, blue suede Le Coq Sportif tennis shoes which you could only get in France.

Socialism

At middle school when we first started playing football competitively, a young PE teacher fresh from college put forward a new way of selecting teams. There was to be no more first or second teams, if you turned up for practise, eventually you'd get a game in the premier eleven. I knew this wouldn't work but had a Socialist spark in me even then and went along with the others. Of course if you don't pick your best players you'll get thrashed every week. As team captain I had to read the match reports out at Assembly. It was incredible the excuses I managed for an eleven-to-three hammering. Playing uphill first half, the wind, the ball not being pumped up enough, the ref being biased. But in the end the teacher himself had to admit our results were the worst in the history of the school. The Headmaster, a keen football man who'd come and watch the odd game himself, demanded an explanation. I sat there while the coach explained his bizarre selection method and smiled as he was overruled. It's strange how this early example of Socialism failing in practise didn't put me off believing in it, in principal, later on. I suppose I was always one for ideals. Cool was an ideal. Hell if you live there.

French Exchange

My exchange Robert had a moped and used to take me round the cafes. His family liked me because I could speak pretty good French; legacy of an international childhood, although I never mentioned this to my French teacher who kept putting me up for awards. Robert's old man had lost a leg in some farming accident and so they all lived off his compensation money. It was weird for me to stay somewhere without central heating and an outside toilet, but you know, it was different, pastoral. The old man took me up to see the war cemeteries. Rows and rows of crosses stretching up and over the horizon. He came here a lot and was really moved by what he called 'the sacrifice' and I felt guilty at feeling nothing. It was a stunning sight, though. Robert and I climbed over the mortar bunkers, trenches. Weaving through the white crosses, the flowers. We could see the old man silhouetted, a wheelchaired figure on the brow of a hill.

Letting off bangers in town at night, the French kids couldn't believe the amount of pleasure we got from this.

Factory

There were no unions, and so you got one ten-minute break about half-twelve for tea and then an half-hour break at two-thirty for lunch. The warehouse was huge and seemed to be split on racial lines. The blacks did all the cleaning, lifting and loading. The whites did the cutting/packing. And the Asians, plus assorted Poles and Turks etc did the nasty stuff with rubber and hot water treatments. I soon figured packing to be the best job and got myself on the A team within a week. If you were quick, neat and showed dexterity with a metal strip you got on packing. If you could do nineteen boxes an hour, which was a record, you got on the A team. This afforded you a position nearer the bog, your own coffee maker, and the ability to qualify for overtime all weekend. This meant you could take home near on three hundred a week if you did two twelve-hour shifts on Saturday and Sunday. I couldn't see the point of working all week and not having time to go out at the weekend; on the A team however, I was the exception. We had Eddie the Greek who never spoke, feeding, Sean the Hell's Angel cutting, and me the Student as they called me, packing. Eddie could feed no end of strip into the tiny gap that served as a runway, laquered the strip and flashed out snakelike to Sean, Stanley knife in hand, who cut them, perfect lengths in one movement and threw them down in front of me. I found the best method was to pick up five at a time, weave them lassoo-like in front of me until I could work them flat. When they were flat I placed them in the box. Each box could take five rows of five but only if they were packed perfectly. If the strips weren't flat enough and you only managed four rows everybody's work rate went down and if it carried over to more than one or two boxes a night, team B would catch up. After you laid a row, then you placed a pre-cut layer of bubblewrap over and started the next row. When you'd done a box, that had to be tied both ends with nasty wired bulldog clips. These had to be tight, not bursting and you had to be careful when you picked them up not to cut yourself. I took part in the stupid competition between teams until one night when we tried to go for the previously unimagined twenty boxes. All of us wanted to reach the golden figure. But Sean had been drinking before coming on shift and in his haste he lopped off the end of his thumb with the Stanley knife. The guy was so cool, he went over to the Coke machine, got some ice, threw the thumb in, got in his own car and drove himself to hospital. Never saw him after, though. Apparently they used his drunkenness as an excuse to keep the incident quiet. I wasn't surprised. Anything but the crazy productivity-equals-overtime equation which forced the accident.

Minicabbing

As I was on one of the firm's cars I earned less than the other drivers, but you could still make a hundred and twenty quid doing the Friday/Saturday night pub circuit. You'd be on the go until about two in the morning, go to this pub, pick them up, take them down the Comrades Club, Boaters, some hotel. Airport pickups were a pain, parking up and all that. Standing there holding a name card. I hated it. Because I was signing, I only wanted to do a couple of nights top-up anyway. So after being started on a few quiet nights I graduated to the weekend. The guvnor would take over the controls then and he was the worst, hot tempered, most short fused controller we had to deal with. If he felt hungry he'd blast down the radio,

Car 5?

POB. (Passenger On Board)

When you drop the passengers off, can you go past the kebab house on your way back? And I'll have a doner, large, with chilly sauce and all the salads. Oh yeah, chips an all. Large and make sure they put plenty of ketchup on them. I'll divvy up with you when you get back.

All this with passengers sitting behind!

Like most of the drivers the guvnor didn't drink so he filled his considerable belly with pies and cakes. He was always sending someone out for something. As soon as anyone complained they were told to bring their radios in. Cab firm shorthand for You're sacked. Drivers came and went. Most were working the second job, just finished at the plant, got home, changed, came and drove until midnight. They had kids to put through school. Fifty-pound trainers to buy. A little evening cash paid for those. There was one other young driver there, who like me was signing but he took the risk of working days, including the one he had to go in on. Told me how he had a scruffy pair of jeans in the back of the cab to change into. Did this striptease in Weybridge car park. Had a scare once, when one of the benefit staff ordered a taxi, he played it cool though, borrowed a hat and shades from the sports shop next door, picked her up, she didn't even look at him. The very woman he'd had his six-monthly review with! Because we didn't have proper insurance, the guvnor gave me a little induction in what to do if the Old Bill pulled you over.

If you're not with a customer, chuck the radio out of the window. If you are. Make 'em get out and leg it. Then ditch the radio.

He was a mad fucker, but no-one ever got pulled over much in Molesey, even if we were the cheapest cab firm on the block and did the pub circuit. The war against other cab firms was continual. I kept clear of this, but every driver had to do his share of carding. This meant if you had a drop near a telephone box you had to make sure our cards were prominently placed and the others were taken out and dumped. I was too cool to bother with this, but the boss was small-minded enough to check any he passed. We had plenty of work. One old lady was a regular. She was what the women controllers called our bread and butter customers. She took the same route everyday. Pick her up at her house at twelve, down The Hand and Spear until closing, then back home. Because her house smelt of cat's piss some of the drivers refused to knock and sat outside beeping. I went up there though, even opened the car door for her. They laughed at this when she commended it to the guvnor, started calling me the Gent, but you know, if you can't respect the old, where are you?

The guvnor respected nothing. He'd sexually harass the

young girls who came and hung around the video machines. Look at those Ruperts! He'd shout, grabbing their breasts as they tried to pull away. He was a master at making it all seem like a little horseplay, nothing serious, but as one of the drivers said to me once, One time he's going to be doing that and his wife will walk in.

She never did and the girls kept coming back. Even the sixteen-year-old he had working the phones tolerated it. Oh he doesn't mean it, she explained. I asked her why she didn't report him. I like this job, she says, better than working Tesco's. All the teenagers who hung round the office were dying to be accepted and join in the male banter between the guvnor and some of his more loyal drivers. One of these, Derek, was trying to better himself by studying technical drawing at night school. The guvnor got no end of pleasure winding him up about this. He put up little How To Draw diagrams around the office and forced Derek to bring in some examples of work which he hung in the TV/coffee area out back alongside the girlie calendars. Occasionally he'd let one of his kids colour them in or write Man United on it. I felt for Derek, whatever he did got laughed at. The guvnor sent him out for a paper once and he bought back the *Daily Mail*.

What's this? Shouted the guvnor, immediately attracting everyone out front. He held up the paper like someone had pissed on it.

It's a paper, said Derek, you asked for a paper I bought you one.

But I want a real paper, the guvnor bellowed, you know, one with tits in it! What do you call this, go on take it back, take it back and get me the *Sun* or the *Mirror* at least. I want to see girls, I want to see tits!

Out went Derek. I must admit this little exchange cracked us all up for varying reasons. For me the *Daily Mail* was worse than any tabloid; at least there was an honesty to their affrontery. The *Mail* was Thatcher's voicebox and spewed out its Falklands nonsense on every page. I kept my political views quiet with the cabbies though, best keep schtum.

The guvnor loved warring with other firms. Ordering hoax taxis, badmouthing their controllers. I don't know why he bothered, nobody was competing with our fares anyway. We were fifty pence lower on most rides than the other minicabs; most of whose drivers refused to do the pub circuit anyway. And as for the station drivers, well they were like royalty to us. Sitting waiting for a train to arrive, luxury. Two pound fifty minimum. That was our average fare, we even had a two pound fare for local trips. I didn't mind this, fitted in with my Socialist ethic, but the other drivers were constantly trying to get prices raised. I can't make ends meet on this! The pub nights were rough sometimes but I never had any real grief, never had any sick to clear up either. Guess I was lucky. I took anybody and went in the pub to look for them, breaking the golden rule of minicabbing; never get out of the car. You had your money belt round your waist, wore slacks: no jeans except on the guvnor's day off, and T-shirts were allowed as long as they were smart ones. Some drivers wouldn't pick people up if they were too far gone, but I found the more pissed they were, the bigger the tip. Another crash stopped me, again not my fault. I was dropping off some customers outside a busy pub and this idiot came roaring by and clipped one of the back doors as it was being opened. The car went skidding through the red light and turned the bend before I could take his registration down. Again old muggins had to pay for a door and back wing pommel/respray. Three hundred quid. I seem to have spent half my adult life paying off car debts and not one of them were for my crashes! Suppose I should be thankful for small mercies. Derek wrote off his Sierra and the car he had a head-on with. Had to pay for both out of his own pocket. Hire and Reward Insurance was high enough without losing your no-claims and as a full-time driver he couldn't afford to. I got a bit disillusioned after my little altercation and got bored with the guvnor hassling me to pay it off. Also the dole people were sending out inspectors to spy on people so I got paranoid about that as well and left. Really, the money you earned outside weekend nights was derisory. I heard stories about firms in Cobham and Ascot where drivers were making a hundred and eighty a night, but you had to have a brand new Volvo or Granada to get those gigs, and I didn't.

Childhood Baggage

I used to be terrified to go to bed. I thought the Devil was speaking to me. He murmured in a low growl; like a madman speaking in tongues. My mother took me to the doctor. At school they recommended psychiatry. My brother and I escaped into the woods. We joined in the stick-fighting with the boys from the village. I was always scared of getting hit in the eye but still aimed at theirs. Between the trees, my brother and I set up a series of trip wires; climbing trunks to get aerial views on those who fell. Squirrels seemed to have the run of the place before we arrived. We stunned them with ball-bearings from our catapults, poured paraffin over their fluffy tails and stood back to strike the match. The heat generated soared up through the body and made the head explode. Bang!

Max

When my little brother Max was born with Down's Syndrome it forced me to look inside myself for the first time. My family had always taken their healthy complexions, lithe physiques for granted. My father had never allowed the pot belly to appear as so many of my friends' fathers had. My mother bears a passing resemblance to Doris Day and we've all inherited her sunny disposition and positive outlook. When Max arrived this didn't change. I was still at school. I remember my father taking my brother and I to one side and explaining that Max was a fine baby boy, it was just that he had a slow brain and would need special attention. Of course a new baby in the house is an excitement whatever and as we didn't really understand what was wrong with him, we accepted we had a younger brother and that was great. My mother's steadfast gaze covered all cracks. I realise the solid front we put up marginalised those in the family who had every right to be upset, shocked, take time out. But in our house the family way ruled supreme. My dad's dad said, He's a Manti and don't you forget it. He'll always be welcome in my house.

I didn't realise the length of time it took Max to learn to eat properly, walk upright, speak basic phrases. It was only when we had other people's kids over that we noticed. Max doesn't look particularly Down's, although I guess everyone thinks that of their kin; but he hasn't the bad heart or behavioural problems of some of his peers. He hated wearing his glasses and constantly threw them across the room. We were supposed to smack him lightly on the hand for this. I found it difficult. Because of his dry skin we took it in turns applying E45 cream every night. Bedtimes were a set procedure; each of us had our task. Suddenly, there were so many things to prepare. I remember telling my friends about Max but there was a general ignorance about the mentally handicapped in those days and most didn't know what to say. Some who said, I'm sorry, would get an earful from me. What's there to be sorry about? He's fine!

Growing up, Max developed curvature of the spine and had to go into hospital for what seemed like months and have rods implanted. We went to see him every weekend in his ward, and there he'd be curled up with his body brace on, drowsy through painkillers. My mother lived with him at the hospital right through it, and we missed her. Her mum came down and looked after us, while Dad was at work, and we liked the fact that Gran made tea at five and we could still go out and play afterwards. Normally dinner happened about seven when my dad came in the door. Max lost some of his fire in the operation; he no longer threw his glasses, but he still had his warm open manner, his dry sense of humour. His speech developed but even now he will fall back on one-word questions and answers if we let him get away with it. I have to invent scenarios when I'm speaking to him on the phone so that he can't just answer Yes or No. When he started school he was picked up at the bus stop in Weybridge near where I hung out with my gang. I fought someone who shouted, 'Look at the Spastic Bus!' When he found out my brother was on it, he grovelled for months. I couldn't see what difference that made. I guess looking back I might have joined in the cheap laughter if it hadn't have been Max. The first time I went out shopping with him I couldn't believe the stares he received in town centres. I used to have a go at people on those occasions also, this of course made it worse, attracted more attention.

Going on a tube was especially uncomfortable. Watching people pretend not to look. Eventually you realise people

only stare out of curiosity. For them Max is unusual, different. Given half a chance, many would praise his stylish hair
and John Lennon glasses.

Max loves to swim and on our summer holidays we often
stayed on sites with big public pools. Anticipating the first
day of going down the pool, showing off our imperfect
family was a trial for me. I recognised how pathetic this was
and insisted I take Max with me. I had my arm round him
and his best friend as we passed the cool crowd, looking for
seats. I can recollect this and know it had nothing to do with
perceived stares from them or any holidaymakers, it was all
about me.

When Max was still small, my mum's dad came to live
with us, and so while I was getting home late, my report card
signed, my mother was cooking for him, cooking later for us,
trying to deal with my older brother's temper tantrums (if
Jack didn't like his dinner he'd throw the plate at the wall) as
well as care for the new baby. I guess my parents didn't have
a lot of free time, and so I shouldn't have expected my father
to turn up and watch football matches as some of the other
fathers did. You still want him to come though. Mum and
Dad came to all my plays. Evening time babysitters and
aupair girls were available. We loved having our grandfather
under the same roof as us, and borrowed his white three
quarter-length raincoat, which was original Mod, without
telling him. Grandad was old school, an English gentleman
who dressed up even if he was popping out for a newspaper.
Hat and walking stick, shirt, tie, waistcoat, jacket, flannels
and brogues. Max loved his stick but wouldn't accept it after
Grandad had died. I guess he knew the accessory dies with
the man. Grandad liked to tell us long stories about Sally Cat,
a character he'd invented who was constantly on the move,
having adventures. Sally Cat shadowed our childhood and
paralleled Grandad's life on the road working as a commer-
cial traveller in fashion. He was a man of charm, charisma
and seeming contradictions. He couldn't see anything wrong
with Max, though once conceded, He's a little slow isn't he?

He voted Liberal yet took the Sun. Thought Margaret Thatcher was great for the country but had no time for the Conservative Party. Jack and I would argue the relative merits of trade unions with him. He'd been in the rag trade; people kept their word then, he claimed. He liked to listen to Friday Night is Music Night and Any Questions. He watched Dallas and Stuart Burrows Sings and feigned an interest in football for our benefit, although living most his life in Southend, he surmised:

Not a football town, Southend, a seaside town. Fit for bowls mostly.

As he slept downstairs, he would let us in if we got back late without our key. He'd keep it a secret. Give us a little wink.

My friends were supportive over Max and many would ask after him. They said I didn't talk about him much, which I suppose was true, but I wasn't avoiding the subject; I just didn't feel like bringing up Down's Syndrome every time family cropped up in conversation. I see now that wasn't what they meant, but you know, when you're young, you're touchy and defensive. We were always big on family loyalty, maybe too big. Max went through school with extra speech tuition and physiotherapy for his back. He never will walk straight, but I don't notice his stooped motion. You don't when you see it every day. To me he's cool. He copies everything I do. I take him out to gigs and stuff, people in London are often surprised to see him at these sorts of event. But why should my brother only go to charity events and musicals? He loves live bands. Why not Sonic Youth at Brixton Academy? He's not listening to the music much though, just looking at the lights and blowing his whistle between songs.

He's twenty-two now and playing in the Special Olympics in Hull at snooker. I suppose I'll have to take back what I said earlier about the family's sporting prowess. He's got a natural flair for potting. Beats me regularly. He lives in a converted country house with his own age group and I see him every other weekend. My parents rightly decided he'd get more stimulation in a shared environment; he was getting bored at home. He goes to college four days a week and learns gardening, sport and lifeskills. For example, they drop off him and a friend in town and get them to get the bus back, use the phone etc. He seems happy enough. He used to go to there for weekends from the age of sixteen; now he comes home for weekends. Although we have to accept that where he lives all week is his home: it is. There was a period of depression and homesickness when he first left but that's something we've all felt. His placid nature and perfect manners are a tribute to my father's patience, teaching him to tie his laces, shave. My mother probably has the hardest time taking him back after a weekend. She usually stays in the house while my father drives him through the darkness of a Sunday night. They share a fascination with numbers and my father has reluctantly become interested in the National Lottery at Max's insistence. Max always goes off to buy his ticket in Woolworth's while he shops in Sainsbury's. Max sits in front of the television at seven-fifty checking the numbers. We often wonder what legal complications would ensue if he won.

Grace

Grace was the first girl at school to dye her hair. She didn't need make up and knew it, lining her eye just a smidgen. When she smiled there were bad teeth at the front, but for me, it made it more of an event. I followed her around; sometimes clinging to her arm. We sat all day in the cloakroom. It was the only place which afforded any privacy. We'd talk, look out the window. She had no energy for study. I guess her IQ was too high. She was one of those that fall into no category. It took us a while to get it together, trying not to stare. Eventually we were thrown that way in Drama. She had to make me up. She touched her thigh against mine as she leaned towards me, paint stick in hand. The teacher made some comment about splitting us up. As I had a slight erection, I blushed. Grace saw that. Smiled.

Grace lived in a big old house by the fire station. Every once in a while, we'd be woken in her bed by the engines. She never failed to jump up and exclaim as they swung round and disappeared down the hill. Her bedroom was small, right at the top, one window. It was sparsely furnished, she didn't seem to have the taste for nick-nacks I'd seen with other girls. We made love for the first time in the sunhouse at the bottom of the garden. We spent a lot of time there, watching her dad water. He was a strange one; like a lodger in his own house.

He'd pick us up from the youth club, never asking anything about what had happened that night. He'd sit at the head of the table for meals, all the action passing him by.

Evenings, he used to watch *Panorama* and smoke a pipe. All the walls were tobacco yellow. I helped him make a rock garden once but he wasn't too impressed. He ended up going over all the bits I'd done. It wasn't like he was a gardener though. He was a retired solicitor. Did real-estate stuff mostly. Would never touch divorce. He liked to remind his wife of this over Sunday lunch.

Are your parents still together? He asked, turning my way.

Sure, I replied, twenty-five years.

Good lad, he'd say, as if it was because of me.

Grace's mother would wear long flowery dresses and harangue her daughter for dressing down.

Why the blacks and browns? You look so gloomy.

All young women today dress in baggy clothing (this was Dad) are they ashamed to be women?

Everyone ignored him. Grace's older brother was part of the drug crowd and flitted in and out. I remember watching him be sick once after simultaneously eating tomato, egg, orange and milk shake. He was dark, scrawny. He used to come in late and sit on the bed with us, offering the joint even though it was always declined. He was nice like that. Manners I suppose. He used to get into bother in pubs and stuff. He was sensitive, shy and potentially annoying if you didn't see he was trying to cover it all with bravado. Grace adored him. Used to pull at his hair like a pet. He went out to Thailand for six months of the year, eventually stayed. Told us how the dealers out there could order their junkies to clean their car for them before handing a fix over. They had such power, he grinned, shaking his head. I didn't know whether he was admiring them or sympathising with the junkie. Grace was pretty sure he dealt. They'd get a lot of phone calls, Friday night. Kids we'd never seen came knocking for him. The house was so big though, everyone could just shut themselves off in their own little world. Grace and I would spend whole weekends in bed. We'd get up, eat, go back. The only time we went out was to the cinema. I'd drive her up to

London, every Monday night. We went to the Swiss Centre, the National, saw some French thing. All arty, black-and-white with subtitles. Grace liked those best. All the women are beautiful, she said. We didn't socialise. I lost touch with my friends outside of college hours. I guessed they were at some pub, some party and I'd been through that. It was what you did when you were single and then all of a sudden Grace followed her brother to Thailand and I was. The last letter I got she was teaching little kids to paint. She said she was happy enough on her own. She went to visit her brother and just decided to stay. She worked two days a week and claimed no-one hassled her for staying in bed the rest of the time. She stressed this as somehow the norm. I doubted this, though she did pity the Westerners who imagined the local girls felt something for them, so maybe it wasn't all drug talk. Why don't you come? She wrote. I missed you when you went to London. What are you doing there? What's happening?

Home Truths

As soon as he saw the Queen, Jack stood at the Christmas table and in front of family and friends turned the television off. My mother asked him to turn it back on, my brother refused. He then blocked my mother's path as she tried to over-rule him physically. By the time my father stepped in (too late as usual) all the shouting and screaming had died down and we'd missed the transmission. My Socialist leanings enabled me to side with Jack in spirit but I would never dream of interfering with my mother's Christmas wishes. After all, even if you viewed the event politically, she was the worker.

After my brother was married, Christmas began to take a turn for the worse. Jack's wife confirmed his yearning for the East (Jain religion in particular) and both were inclined to meditate just as dinner was being served. Coming back in, the newly-weds held up proceedings even more by stringing out grace to include a prayer, a long poem, and then going round the table asked each guest what the occasion meant to them. Needless to say, a couple of us tucked in, ignoring their rudeness, and received a volley of abuse.

Are you really so shallow? Is Christmas so meaningless? Is food so important?

It is when it's hot, I said.

My father, ever accommodating after the rod of iron his own father had employed, said little. My mother fumed, her creation ruined. During the meal the conversation turned inevitably and somewhat embarrassingly for Jack and I, to the subject of employment. Less so for my brother this year, however, as he'd been working at Selfridges and was considering the prestigious management training course. Before his marriage, he'd been an artist for years and had never managed to hold down a full-time job. I still had this status. My father was a little taken aback when Jack informed him that he had prepared the ground for his possible promotion by coming clean about his initial application. To get the job, he'd done a bit of creative writing on his curriculum vitae to cover up the years he spent painting. Naturally, we all stated, in the current job climate, everyone does it! This didn't satisfy my brother, his new-found zeal for personal advancement didn't extend to what he saw as accepting lies. Yes, my father argued, but we all cover gaps in our applications. You're obviously going to promote the best aspect of yourself, otherwise you'd never get an interview! My brother listened with patience and then began to quiz my father about what untruths he'd written on his original CBI form. My father had worked for the multi-national all his life and couldn't recollect that far. He'd done his National Service, learned a trade and was in the right place at the right time when he came out. They recruited him.

See! Shouted Jack, You didn't lie.

My father tried to soften the blow by claiming he would have done if he had to; but my brother was off then.

Just before the Christmas break, he recounted to the horrified looks of my family and the unbelieving upturned half-smile on my face, I went to my superior and informed him of the lies on my original application. I took with me a true list of all colleges I'd attended, the jobs I'd been sacked from, the exams I'd retaken rather than just passed...

Somehow my father remained calm.

What did he say?

He told me not to worry about it, said he's done the same, told me it would go no further.

See? My father triumphed.

Jack looked disappointed, grew solemn.

I've chosen this Christmas to tell you everything, he declared, as you might be aware my brother-in-law has been made the youngest manager of USBANK in the history of the company!

Ignoring the purrs of approval, Jack turned to me.

What's wrong with us two? Why did we go through that pathetic teenage rebellion stage? Look where we could have been if we hadn't wasted so much time!

Yeah but we had a laugh didn't we? I shrugged. Who wants to be a bank manager anyway, I thought but didn't say it. Christmas wasn't the occasion to voice such sentiments.

Jack then turned to my parents. Do you see those Christmas presents under the tree? This is not only the first year I have bought them with my wife but up until a few years ago the first time I have bought them ever.

How do you mean? Quizzed my mother.

When Slim and I gave joint presents we stole every one!

I choked on my turkey. Tried to laugh it off. I softened the claim by launching into the old, Well we all go through shoplifting phases in our teenage years... My gran, who saw the positive in everything, began a story about the propensity of theft in her sheltered accommodation this Christmas. Her tone implied catching a thief had cheered the place up no end. I could see Jack tensing up. He'd long held the conviction that I was the family favourite; the golden boy who could do no wrong while his efforts (his paintings in particular) were shunned. I felt the praise I got stemmed from academic achievements and wouldn't hesitate for a second to state we both got the same love and affection growing up. If anything Jack's volatile temperament (under a common cold he'd become delirious; he'd occasionally sleepwalk) secured him more of my parent's time.

It was painful for me to witness my older brother make this yearly exhibition of himself. I hardly saw him now, outside of family occasions. We'd grown up close, brothers who became best friends, we'd shared a flat throughout our college years, papering its walls with our poems and paintings...

Then one summer, while walking in the Alps, Jack had a religious experience. He saw himself, in a former existence, as a hermit living in a cave on the edge of a gorge. The revelation changed him. Jack had always been attracted to ascetic codes of behaviour and when he returned from the mountains, his fundamentalism grew in direct proportion to his intolerance at my agnosticism. He began to live the life of that hermit he saw in the vision. I never doubted that something had happened that day but I wasn't there. It didn't apply to me. If at this Christmas table I'd dared to suggest that perhaps this was neither time nor place for a confessional he might rightly have stated this was exactly the time and place.

If not on Christ's birthday, when? What are you scared of Slim?

Well…

Jesus told the truth and look what happened to him.

Next up came the time Jack and I made a tidy profit selling copies of the church magazine to unsuspecting locals innocent of the fact the magazine was complimentary. We hid behind the congregation one Sunday and stole a fair pile, knocked on doors and asked twenty pence an issue. We made enough to enjoy a Wimpy Kingsize and International Grill to spoil our appetites for Sunday lunch on the way home. Jack claimed to recall the exact amount we extorted, then announced he had put that sum in the collection box at last night's Midnight Mass.

This story shocked the family a little but they took the view that as we were never caught and made some money perhaps we'd shown some initiative. Grandmother was especially excited.

No-one said you couldn't sell the leaflets!

And by selling them we might have encouraged more people to go to church! I added. My mother gave me a wry smile. I had gone too far. I was the only family member absent from last night's service. Desperation was starting to show. I had some nasty secrets about my brother up my sleeve and figured I might drop one in, first strike, you could say, if this got any worse. Jack then added, in all seriousness, that if the vicar 'hadn't been so busy last night' he would have stood up and confessed the deception in front of the whole congregation as some of those present might well have been the deceived.

Full compensation would have been meted out, no doubt? Queried my father, warming up. My brother nodded earnestly.

Thankfully the Christmas pudding arrived and we began the toasts. Jack had always loved toasting obscure celebrities in the past and here, finally, his sense of fun returned. After a moment of seriousness when he explained why he now toasted Gandhi instead of Winston Churchill, we proceeded into the long list of minor media figures which always brought the family together in laughter and good cheer. Jack and I took it in turns whilst younger brother Max interjected Cheers! after every name. The roll call began…

Roald Dahl, Sacha Distel, Elvis, Derek Jarman, Mother Teresa, Cindy Crawford…

It wasn't long before my brother's and his wife's eccentricities got them banned from the family Christmas. I couldn't blame my parents. Some home truths are best left.

Sorting Mail

You had to fill out a form to say if you were prepared to drive a van to pick up mail (yes) drive a push-bike and deliver mail (no) or work nights in the sorting depot (double yes). I got the job. It seemed like everyone who applied did. The warehouse was filled with the dregs of the earth – teenagers who could hardly speak, students, Asian mother and daughter teams in saris – all lined up in front of their allotted sixteen pigeonholes, all with postcodes on. Every couple of hours the man came round and took out a stack of envelopes to check you'd sorted them properly. If you fucked up on more than one or two they put you on tying up bags. I was quick and had a good throw though, so I was all right. We did twelve-hour shifts with short breaks for tea, coffee. There was nowhere to go. They had a machine for drinks and confectionery, some chairs… The shift ended at six in the morning and the air was a hazy grey as you walked to the train station and home.

My first night I made the mistake of assuming the work would be done in silence (why hadn't I learned from my other warehouse jobs?) – I guess I was expecting the sorting rooms to be isolated and not part of the general chaos of bags, vans pulling in and out etc – but no, I had to suffer an entire night of the Capital Radio playlist, round and round the same old tunes at full volume. I nearly quit there and then but as I knew my Walkman would save me the next night I stayed. Good old Sony! The song of that yuletide was Ini Kamoze's, 'Here Comes the Heartstopper – Murderer!' and whenever this came on an idiot who I assumed the first night was a supervisor or something (he would walk round chatting everyone up and ruin the silence of tea break by asking everyone, 'How's your first night? Liking it then?') – Anyway this guy loved Ini Kamoze and whenever the chorus came round he would sing it at the top of his lungs. The playlist being as it is 'Here comes the Heartstopper!' would come round countless times in the twelve hours and he never tired of it.

The job was okay, they gave you a stool-cum-perch which some chose to sit on while sorting but I found it hurt my back and so did all my throwing standing up. Occasionally I'd try flash throws like spinning and chucking them over my shoulder and some of the other temps were upset by this and claimed it put them off, but their slowness made them powerless to do anything about it.

Pick up an envelope, see the code – throw! I don't know how many I did an hour but it seemed like a lot. It didn't matter that much – we were being paid an hourly wage unrelated to productivity – but I had to keep my hit ratio high so as to avoid the bags. The sing-song idiot would spend all night going round geeing everyone up, 'loving it!' he was, 'mad for it!' The second night I saw him clocking in with the rest of us and went over to the woman at the desk. I picked her out as a rare person my first night and we'd built up quite a rapport. She confirmed my suspicions.

'Him a manager? No,' she smiled. 'He wants to be.'

I planned my revenge at tea break. I had just sat down, turned off my Walkman, when over he came.

'Don't like Capital Radio then?'

'No,' I said.

'What you listening to?'

'Oh, you know, this and that,' I said. I always tried to make it easy for these people. Give them a way out. They never took it. Sing-song leapt towards me and tried to grab the tape from my Walkman, I parried him with my free arm.

'Don't fucking touch me,' I shouted, 'ever!'

'All right, calm down!' He protested, 'If it was any good I was going to put it on you know… it plays tapes that machine as well.'

I said nothing.

He sat down. Looked my way.

'How you finding it then? On your second night… you fitting in all right?'

That did it. I cracked.

'Listen cunt! You're not a manager so stop swanning around as if you run the place and any of us give a shit. It's a Christmas job get it? We do the hours then we fuck off. We don't give a fuck about fitting in, or the Royal Mail, get it?'

I'd said 'We' but looking round all the other temps were as stunned at my outburst as he was. His chin nearly hit the floor and for a minute I thought he was going to cry. I nearly felt for him then. Maybe he'd been out of work for a while and was just pumped up and excited. I felt a smidgen of guilt. Not enough to apologise, though.

Sing-song stopped singing after that. The bird had flown.

The problem with sorting Christmas mail is there's no end to it – no job satisfaction – for as soon as you've made some headway along comes the man and dumps another pile on. I learnt one thing though – always write the postcode large and clear – that way one glance and it's sorted. No postcode and you had to look up these sheets pinned to the wall, breaking your rhythm. I knew most the roads in the area I'd been given from my minicab days and so didn't have to hit the wall much but most the other temps loyally went back and forth all night! If in doubt, guess, was my motto. I've never been a great one for accuracy and any average I might have accumulated my rebel nature would subvert anyway. I had to throw a couple deliberately wrong each night, just to keep Big Brother on his toes.

After my second week a permanent member of staff, a driver, took me to the subsidised canteen at Surbiton. He claimed it was a reward for my efforts – Christmas dinner on the house – for the fastest gun in the warehouse. I'd managed to bolt down a couple of mince pies before the inevitable Christmas career chat began.

'You're a good sorter, kid. You could earn a mint.'

To keep the pain minimal, I decided to set him straight.

'I only took the job because it was temporary. That way I can sign back on again once it's over.'

'Why do you want to do that?'

'I'm a writer. I need the time.'

He paused.

'I thought there was something going on in that head of yours. What do you do for beer money?'

'It's got to be cash,' I explained, 'this place is legit, isn't it?' I looked round. 'Everyone's on the books?'

'Anything wrong with that?'

'Not at all,' I defended. 'I probably wouldn't hate it but there are things like the uniform, you know... '

'The uniform!' He was astonished.

'Yeah, I couldn't wear it.'

'Why not?'

'I don't know. It's just me. I have these things I can't do. Like I can't do cleaning jobs, even though most of them are cash. Don't ask me why.'

'Pride?' He offered.

We shared a smile.

The driver was a good sort. He wished me luck. He knew that people needed something to read on the train, on their way into work. He knew they needed to turn on the television at the end of the day and have programmes to watch, and where did they think they came from? From us, me, writers – that's where!

Near the end the management came down and mucked in for about five minutes and we were all supposed to be impressed as they took their jackets off and rolled their sleeves up. One bright spark decided to sort next to me.

'You're good at that aren't you?' He encouraged.

'I was basketball champ at school,' I said, showing him one of my throws.

'Were you really?' He enthused.

'No.'

He couldn't believe his ears. The bell went. Saved by it again. The woman behind the desk gave me my cheque and a beatific smile. That was Christmas. The cheque they gave us was Girobank, I was used to these, queue up at the Post Office, tick the box on the back before scribbling your signature underneath. By paying me that way it was almost like they were trying to tell me something. 'Go on son, you're doing the right thing, you'll make it!' I signed back on in the New Year, a stretch of writing before me.

Letter To America

How to write of that summer? I keep trying to start with the phone call to say you were coming over with some idiot I'd never heard of, who eventually pulled out – thank God, because as you said later, he could never have handled us two together. The call which came while I was out working; can you believe it? Six-week stint I did minicabbing, as I needed spending money for the trip. Ring, ring went the phone and the girl I was seeing took the call and got all excited as she was American and so wanted to meet my American best friend. And when you came over she took a real shine to you – love, she called it, and even dragged her hand against a wall or something, some passionate thing, after you left. So in a matter of hours, I'd faked a tennis injury to get off work, kicked the American girl out of my flat, and all in time for your arrival! She stayed nearby. Pretty neat, huh!? You came through customs with your tough haircut and wearing the shades you would adopt for the whole trip, hiding alcoholic eyes. And we spent a few days in London, staying with Bill and coming home drunk with you sleeping on the bathroom floor. Bill's flat in King's Cross which at the time was chock-a-block with artists and East Europeans, had a roof-top balcony overlooking Caledonian Road. Bill would sit in his deck chair, holding forth, while Hendrix or The Pixies blasted through giant speakers facing out.

On our second night we went to party, seeing Annie Anxiety at The Venue, New Cross. Both astonished to catch an organised coach back to Leicester Square. Anxiety is the dizziness of freedom, you kept telling everyone on the coach, but you weren't anxious or dizzy enough to sleep at Bill's again, so I knocked up an old girlfriend at two in the morning, who lived in an exclusive address with a cold ice-pick of a flat mate. Standing by her intercom, I sold her some story about falling out with my brother who lived nearby as a precursor. Going in, I told you I'd sleep with her, you know, it'd be rude not to, and you looked at me drunkenly and said Yep! Which was so meaningless we both laughed. And there she was, greeting us in her pyjamas and she had that slight Italian look you always liked, and you generously offered to sleep with her if I didn't want to. I laughed at this while we drank gin in the kitchen and said, No you don't know her, she's not that type of girl. In I went.

The next morning she woke us at some ungodly hour as she had to go to work and her ice-queen of a flat mate certainly didn't want us watching Richard and Judy with her. So we hobbled our way down to the tube and you smoked while I nodded along with her talk of work and responsibilities. The business people on the platform made me edgy and I started cracking inane jokes. In the Coach and Horses we had our first drink of the day and you kept saying how the summer should be important, and how you would have ended yourself in that Philadelphia apartment if you hadn't used the drink as a crutch. I noticed the drinking of course, but felt like I was the only one who wasn't going to tell you to stop. I'd just spent six weeks on the wagon, taxi-driving, you know, not wanting to mix it; and was thirsty enough for a drink programme to leap on yours.

Why I suggested the trip to Nice, I don't know. Every summer for the past five years I'd been going down. Staying with my parents in Villeneuve Loubet, taking in some Riviera sunshine, trying to write. The trip down was full of complications, I was getting a free lift with some friends of my father, while you were following on the train later. I thought I could get you on the van but they wouldn't have it. Stupidly, I went alone. Eighteen hours we drove, taking it in turns at the wheel. I was allotted the worst times, the worst stretches of road. I did the Peripherique while they cruised open motorway, 2pm Lyon time. You, Chet, came later; stayed with Louis, our mutual friend and as he was driving you round the Lake District, this took some of my guilt off leaving. On my ride, we stopped over in Montpellier with the van owner and his wife, who had once been my English teacher, but was now a full-time potter. Her kiln going all day. They had a villa in Pouget, with a vineyard and backdrop to the mountains. We drank wine for breakfast and I got up early and never once felt drunk. The few days I stayed, waiting for my parents to come pick me up, went surprisingly well. Long days I spent, lying in a hammock, reading from their library before a supper of olive salads and barbecued meat. The home wine kept coming and I was in a perpetual heaven that couldn't last. A bad night did come, but thankfully, towards the end. A teacher friend of my hosts came over and discussed her recent trip to Africa with one of the businessmen I drove down with. Both parties had been to Africa and knew what they were talking about. I had not. But in my drunken state I insisted on agreeing with the businessman, as his points about Africans being lazy and not understanding irrigation seemed so outrageous. The teacher fighting the other corner either didn't know I was playing Devil's Advocate or didn't care and began telling me to shut up every time I spoke. She was dead right, but after the drink, I had to stay and keep injecting my pathetic little witticisms. Something went off, I can't remember what.

The next day my parents showed. With them around I behaved and it wasn't long before we left Pouget and I was meeting you at the train station in Nice. You came off, wearing the infamous shades and sober and elated, told me of the long poem you'd written on the way down about your parent's alcoholism. You said it was a hard poem for you to write but now you'd written it, you were glad. Later you left me your journal of that summer and I read the poem which began with these lines:

My alcoholism blooms in total darkness, an evil flower. I cannot escape.

Of all differences between us that summer Chet, I guess the main one was the drinking. I'd always like a drink but there was nothing compulsive, no family history of abuse to turn it into something serious, something self-destructive. In the South Of France the alcohol never stopped. My mother organised a succession of early lunches for us to attend with all her art-loving friends. They wanted to embrace the two young writers with abundant hospitality and carafes of wine. Midday we began by sipping Pimms and strawberries, then came the food, the inevitable wine, then a hallucinogenic dip in the heated pool. Then more punch, some beer we'd stolen as chaser, then coffee, brandy, liqueur chocolates... All through lunch you entertained the ladies with tales of how when you'd finished studying at your Ivy League college you would then go into publishing, eventually putting out a series of Slim's (my) work. At this they all Hoorayed! This was the kind of talk they liked to hear and you knew how to lay it on. No talk of near suicide in a Philadelphia apartment block, no talk of how this very trip was being payed for by next term's tuition fees.

And the time you flicked your burning cigarette butt over the balcony, and my father jumped at you, saying you should go down and watch that, make sure it doesn't set light to the dry wood below. I knew he was right, and I knew about the fires all along the coast that summer but for some reason I couldn't get worked up about it. If anything came to symbolise our trip that summer, the casually flicked cigarette was it.

At siesta, we took the sweltering walk to the station, boarded a train for Antibes, and tried to find a shaded café. After café créme, we strolled past the museum, the old town.

We should never have come, I said. I should never have allowed it, I was thinking.

You took an easy bench and watched the waves as I looked at sunlight streaming through strange sculptures on the museum wall.

Look, let's get to Paris. Re-group.

But the day was Friday and you couldn't afford the train trip back until we found a bank which would cash a rather dubious cheque you had. My father kindly agreed to drive us around the banks of Antibes on the Monday. That night we hitched our way to the nearest town as we had every evening. Wherever the driver was headed became our destination. We made our way from bar to bar, and it never failed to amaze how we got picked up and taken home. You suggested we might try it all the way to England as our luck was in, but wanted to see Paris and I had to be back within ten days to sign on. We got lifts from a man who loved his football and eulogised on Gascoigne and Platt, another who loved BB King, others who took us to bars and parties and once to a rave in Cannes, with bands, beer and fireworks overhead. There I met a girl from Liverpool and she clearly wanted me to step out with her, but we'd been slamming back tequila by then and my shouting put her off. On the beach, I walked into the sea fully clothed. You dragged me to the Croisette and right in front of the Opera House you stuck out your thumb half-heartedly and as if wonders never cease! Some tourist in a Dodge van let us jump in the back.

Do you remember those Japanese girls we picked up in that club, the Voom-Voom? Why mine went outside with me I'll never know. I was so drunk I couldn't close my eyes to kiss her. I went round the corner to be sick, lying that I had a telephone call to make. When I came back and kissed her she didn't even flinch at my vomit breath. After spending the night in their hotel, her friend arranged for us all to meet for lunch. I didn't want to go but you went. I was swimming back at the estate with my little brother, thinking, Why can't I relax, go with the flow?

That night you returned late. Said you couldn't face walking on the hot sand. Said she was trying to trap you into marriage. Every new girl you seemed to feel for instantaneously. I took that as part of your condition. There I sat, experimenting with a way of revealing but not revealing too much in the same stroke. Touching a woman's thigh as if my boldness were on account of the all-pervasive night fire flickering, rather than the pounding in my heart.

On Monday we went round the banks. They all took one look at the cheque and shook their heads. My dad couldn't believe it. As we waited for our train, Chet turned to me and asked why my father didn't go straight to his bank and cash that cheque first time. Didn't he realise it was the only way we'd get the money? Rather than shove my fist in your mouth I said it wasn't his problem.

On the train ride home, our cheer was heightened considerably by a young French girl travelling with her family in the next compartment. She kept the sun shining as we entered darkened tunnels, coastal-tracking our way towards Marseilles. Passing the beach where Picasso was photographed riding an elephant, we amused the French girl with our surreal humour. Chet stretching himself after a whole year of French classes in Philly. Later giving up in Paris when *personne* would understand him. And that poem you wrote describing her as 'the embodiment of beauty.' Well you were certainly taken by her, but I, worried about her fourteen years and her father hovering, stepped back a little. When they got off at Marseilles, the father came over and shook our hands – so I shouldn't have worried – and she pecked us on both cheeks and I wanted to cry. Pathetic huh? But in that kiss I felt what I had lost these years. Stupidly we ran out of beer as the sky darkened and had to wait an agonising hour for the train bar to open. During this time, we introduced ourselves to two English women who had entered our carriage. In the train bar I made a big mystery over why we were stopping in Paris. I claimed we had to pick up a 'package' and as both of us looked tired and unshaven from days of what could have been drug abuse, the ladies were happy to swallow all. You were fine about playing along with the whole drug plot they eventually dragged out of us. And as the night wore on, we partnered off. I made a physical play at mine in the corridor, while you looked at photos of something with yours. And whereas mine pushed me away at first, later they both went off, had a little talk, and came back far more enthusiastic. So much so, that though we'd given up and bedded down for the night, in they came and jumped on us. What followed was hours and hours of rolling around on the train floor, and an incident in the toilet where I managed to sit her on the sink and stick a soapy finger up her behind. Later, with her on top, I watched a women's basketball game being played at two in the morning in some God-forsaken French industrial wasteland. It seemed the driver wanted to watch the match, so for an hour we got on with our business with the train no longer rocking beneath us.

We left them at Paris and headed off to find Jim Morrison's grave as planned. All summer we'd been playing that live Doors tape and now we were going there. But in the chain-smoking daze we couldn't remember the name of the cemetery and spent hours wandering round the wrong one. Paris didn't really change us. We went to one café and had a row with the owner who insisted we eat as well as drink. As we had just begun a dialogue with two French girls we put up a struggle before being thrown out. The girls laughing as I shrugged my shoulders instead of protecting your fall against those bins. Staying in the Rue Mouffetard at a hostel for five pounds a night, we found the Café des Artistés etc. You wanted me to teach you to box but I couldn't remember the word for 'gym' in French so we never did. That night ended in the Irish Bar, opposite our dorm, where we persuaded the musician to play covers and embarrassed ourselves in front of two American aupairs by singing along. Again I ended up with the dark one and you the blonde, just like on the couchette; usually it was vice versa. Maybe the confusion caused you to try and kiss my girl that night, but we were both drunk and I hadn't helped break your fall outside that café so…

You fell, feeling the same way now.

The aupairs led us back to their basement. Their employers were sleeping above and we'd promised to be quiet. What was that promise? I shouted, tripping over something. They couldn't see what was so funny and threw us out. We staggered back to the hostel, over an hour walking; and as the owner had gone to bed we had to keep hammering on the door to be let in. He wasn't exactly chuffed to see us at three in the morning, but left us to climb into our bunks and crash. The next day we went to the Rodin museum to look at the work of Camille Claudel. We'd both seen the film the previous year. I went into the shop and bought a ten-by-eight still of Camille in her twenties. It's a famous black and white shot but I left it in the bar we went in afterwards as well as my notebook from the trip. Walking back, the last two French girls we met in Paris were underage, out late and trying to get me to admit to being French despite my thrusting of a British passport under their noses. They were so young, I had to enter a café to buy them cigarettes. One of them kept shouting that if I didn't stop lying she'd go get her dad to come sort me out. Apparently a local gendarme. I couldn't see what she was getting so worked up about. Later you said it was because some people are more convincing lying than telling the truth. They certainly get more practise.

On the train ride to England there was one further incident when you wanted to speak to two Canadian girls and I just wanted to sleep. But you got all sulky so I agreed to have a look and then annoyed you even more by pronouncing them: not worth it. I wanted to sleep, for Christ's sake! Just for five minutes. Okay? If you want to speak to a couple of homely Canadian girls completely out of their depth in Gay Paris go ahead! Just leave me out of it! That's enough madness! I'm going to sleep!

In England you headed south to stay in Brighton with the girl you met on the train, while I went up west to stay with Bill in London. We went out and saw *Terminator 2* at the Empire, Leicester Square. I enjoyed some of it, although I'm not sure about all this Arnie as post-modern great actor bit. His voice still sounds shit to me. Bill kept insisting that was the joke. After I left London and was installed in the flat my gran let me use in Weybridge, you came back from Brighton with a broken foot and a leather jacket, courtesy of her. The foot incident was pretty funny. You, embarrassed at throwing up in a nightclub basin, got so angry at wasting all that alcohol you kicked a wall with your foot and snap it went. My gran lived with her boyfriend in a mobile home. They preferred to live simply. He didn't like the flat. She was a great woman who had once danced professionally and loved the arts enough to encourage my lifestyle, occasionally arranging loans. Her boyfriend, a man she met at dancing class, loved his opera and sometimes sat to a five-hour Wagner without budging. He liked us, bought us beer, told war stories. Told us how when they dropped the bomb on Hiroshima, he and his comrades cheered. Not for the bomb, but for the fact they didn't have to go fight the Japanese. The only good thing about Weybridge is its pubs. At the Grotto we met a French painter staying with an Iraqi in St George's Hills. And you Chet, loved meeting an Iraqi so close to the Gulf War. She was rich and her father was a successful artist no less, though we never met him as he was abroad. I hooked up with the French painter who was over on some kind of exchange programme. She worked with the Iraqi on her father's art; cuddly toys he sold for thousands. From Paris, she was, couldn't handle her drink – which was unfortunate around us – and though I didn't get this art, I didn't say anything. I consider my collection of golliwogs more interesting.

The house they lived in was like a palace, with a studio as big as a basketball court and all these works-in-progress everywhere. One painting where anyone could add anything they chose as long as they signed and dated it on the back. You wrote some lines of poetry, while I added a couple of slashes. The French girl caught me signing a false name on the back and couldn't get over it. Why, Slim? Why do you do that? You know I know your name. I fed her some garbage about a nom-de-plume but she didn't buy it. The night she stayed over at the flat she insisted on keeping her clothes on all night; boots and all! And there I was lying next to her, pathetically trying to pry open her trousers with her so drunk she didn't know where she was. Every day we were back at the house, eating and drinking from the well-stocked kitchen, taking the dad's BMW down to the store where he had an account, loading up, driving back. Other Iraqis came over, studied us, and began to complain about the smoke in the studio. You rightly claimed it wouldn't affect the paint, but she was adamant; kept asking Why? You saying, I smoke because I want to die or something equally facile until she organised a gang of friends/family to throw us out. The French girl, ruined by drink after about two glasses, at this point tired of me trying to kiss her. In the studio we were, her vomiting and throwing glasses at me. In the car with all these cousins around, out she came all doe-eyed and apologetic and will she see me again? Doubt it, I said. Away we drove. All she missed was Eddie Cheever at the Bass Clef and I for once didn't drink. Somehow, the horror of the past weeks got to me in the music and without drink I couldn't keep my sadness in. The two women sitting behind us left before we could buy them one and so home I drove; like a psycho, way too fast, and later you said you were thinking, Okay, if Slim wants us to die tonight I'm prepared for it.

The next morning the American girl who had been staying with me at the beginning of all this called unexpectedly and we both decided as she liked you more (obvious) you should go with her. I drowned my sorrows watching *River's Edge* and *Heathers* on video so many times I knew the lines. And so it was days of me picking you up for drinking bouts, and nights of me dropping you back for her. You'd excuse yourself daytime to go 'do some writing' and then we'd go, pub to pub, off-licence to video shop and back. She wanted to come for the ride but I would never let her. It was some bizarre form of self-loathing/jealousy. After all, I'd been seeing her on the quiet for over a year and didn't even like her.

The next day you left, and I worried about you leaving and you worried about having nothing to go back to, and how the phone would be cut off, and how everything might be cut off. And it all came down to a late afternoon in St James' Park, where we wanted to sleep, but couldn't. There we sat, after an all-dayer at the Scala cinema. And we tried to clear our heads and not smoke nor drink and sit with ducks and swans and try to look at the water in St James's Park. But the water was a blur. Wavy, but not wavy like water (there was no wind) – more like a television screen. Wavy like the broken screen of an insomniac, sounding out its one-note dawn chorus. Its wake up call! I kept thinking I'd fallen asleep on the couch again, but it was a bench. I couldn't move. The buzz kept coming. I couldn't even say:

Chet, don't do it man. Just don't. I love you but it doesn't seem enough.

Razor

Slim Manti and Chet King met due to the closeness of their shaving mirrors. You were the only other student in halls to wet shave using an old fashioned razor. Yours dropped and reflected up to mine, bending down to pick it up. Diamonds glittered like that for us the day she entered the breakfast hall with the wall-length windows. We were sitting with our backs to the sun, discussing the day ahead, when suddenly, in she came. And as she walked towards us, the light caught those green eyes of hers, and there we were, stuck, obsessed. We couldn't move. Ria Diamonds! Even her name was magical. A woman we hardly knew became a paragon of virtue. We'd follow her, the merest movement an invitation, the merest smile; a glimpse of Heaven. The shared obsession sealed our friendship. I did kiss her once, and imagine she was surprised I didn't invite her back to my room, but those rooms were more like prison cells and I was hardly going to de-robe Helen of Troy and slip her slender toga in my slop bucket.

And when I came over for Thanksgiving week not even sure if I would see you Chet, but hoping it was possible, I rung from the Vanderbilt YMCA in Manhattan, only to be told there was no Chet King listed at the address I had. This set the tone for the whole trip. I was in New York to make a film I'd written about a guy who wanders around Greenwich Village until he meets a girl with red hair. He kisses the girl and that's it. Fin. The rich film society at my university had agreed to finance me and a camera crew to go to New York and... We had ten days, but it took the cameraman three to show, and the girl with red hair who was supposed to be coming down from Dartmouth never did. Someone had assumed it was a twenty-minute bus ride for her, confusing New York State with City! I blamed the producer who was paranoid about the expensive equipment and getting mugged and refused to go along with my idea of filming it as it was written ie have me walk around until I did find some-one with the necessary hair tone and get the shot of me kiss-ing her by bribery or just risking it. You'll be done for sexual assault, he shouted, and I'm not going to be an accessory after the fact! I pleaded with the crew that this was one of those times in life when you throw caution to the wind and not care about rules and percentages; but they sided with the producer and went off to film his cousin's Jewish wedding. Before leaving the producer was kind enough to lend me the money to get a Greyhound and go see Chet in Ohio.

All the way down I kept explaining to these black guys sitting on the bus about the girl with red hair. About how if we'd had the belief we would have found her. All they kept saying was: Word.

Look! If I had met the girl with red hair she would have listened to me right? Because I was the writer and she would have seen the passion behind the idea and realised not only would she let me kiss her, but she would enjoy it too?

Word.

And by kissing her we would have been joined somehow and the illusion would not have been shattered but somehow completed...

Word.

And in that coming together we would have symbolised Hope for all men and women down the ages.

Symbols. Word.

Men and women. Word.

That one word seemed to cover all bases, every nuance. At first I thought they were just blanking the white man, but I noticed they said it to each other and it wasn't offered in any rude way, just given out like something soothing. Don't worry, they seemed to be saying, for everything can be cured with Word. Every problem solved. Every impossibly difficult mathematical equation can be cancelled out in one beautiful, clean pronouncement.

When I got to Kent, some hours later, the black guys cheered as I left and pointed to the snow and my ripped trainers and cheap flying jacket: a laughable collection! And waving goodbye and not really believing I was in Ohio, I went to the nearest store and showed them the address. Astounded that I was only two blocks away, I began to walk. The temperature was well below freezing and I knew if I didn't find Chet's house quickly, I'd lose toes from frostbite. I found the house but started banging on the wrong door and woke the landlord, who worked nights and had just got to sleep. He pointed me to the right door and then it came. The first meeting in two years, my hair long then and blowing across my face, and Chet came to the door, squinting in contact, hair dyed black and suddenly we both yelled and danced around in the snow. I showered while he made coffee and then I retold the girl with red hair saga. Chet must have connected that with Diamonds, who was a four-state road trip away in Minneapolis. After the car, our one and only hindrance was the address. Neither of us could remember it, nor did we have a recent letter to check a hunch against. We weren't going to let that stop us, so as soon as we got a car organised, we went. We stopped at the local store to get petrol and stock up on cigarettes, chocolate. We had two years to catch up on, and while we talked we both tried desperately to remember Diamonds' address. Don't think about it, we'd say, and it will come. We knew it was Minneapolis, Minnesota but that was about it. Another problem aside from the destination was our travel fatigue. I had just spent the entire night talking and wording with those New York brothers and Chet, unprepared for my arrival, had slept badly the night before, and though we both took it in turns at the wheel there was no way we were going to drive through the night and make it. We got to about Chicago when the trouble started. I was driving while Chet tried to take a little nap, but he wasn't allowing himself any real rest as he had to keep an eye on me driving his dad's station wagon and trying so hard to stay awake I kept punching myself in the face. I had the car running with the white lines in between the wheels as I wanted their intensity to keep me awake. Chet thought that was how we drove in England and kept saying, If you drive in the middle like this we'll be stopped!

I must have dropped off because when I woke up it was glaring morning and Chet had wrapped blankets round us and parked the car in an endless field of white. I got out and walked about in the frozen wastes and felt so good and strong in this barbaric ice-cap that I looked out at America for the first time. Tried to find my place in it.

At the New Day café we emptied the car ashtray and had a cooked breakfast of scrambled egg, hash browns and pancakes. Chet said we'd be in Minneapolis by mid-morning if I was okay to drive. I was and thought by taking the wheel my memory might be jogged concerning the still-elusive address. Then as we drove up the main causeway to the city something came into my head about Innsbruck.

Innsbruck, I said, where's that?

Sounds like somewhere in Eastern Europe, Chet joked.

In the city we went to a big hotel and asked if we could look at their street map. They looked up Innsbruck and sure enough there it was. Innsbruck Parkway in St Paul. Off we went then, we had the road, we didn't have the number. For some reason I thought it was a four-digit number but this turned out to be a red herring. You had the sensible idea of going into a bar and looking the name up in the phone book, but there was nothing listed. Private number, we surmised. We were reduced to driving up and down a long snow-covered road and trying to guess. The lengths of invention you go to when squeezing crumbs of this importance from your used-up mind! It was killing us and our powers already weak, sure enough, we chose the wrong house. But this road trip will reach its destination as the old chap who answered was Chairman of the Innsbruck Parkway Residents Association and though didn't know the Diamonds in question, just happened to have a list of all family properties and was happy to proffer us the number. He trusted the Englishman with this vital piece of information and back we went to what turned out to be the first house in the road! We'd driven past it umpteen times.

As no-one was home we sat in the car and waited. After about ten minutes Diamonds' mother turned up and was hospitality personified, inviting us to wait for Diamonds' return from work. We sat and chatted and had tea and cake and I played the piano while Chet slumped back, shattered but rejuvenated by our triumph. The mother insisted she not call Diamonds but leave it as a surprise. This, at the time, gave me a bad feeling and sure enough when Diamonds did return, hours later, she had boyfriend Kevin in tow. Now Kevin had struggled for months to get parents and two other daughters alike to accept him into the hearth. But for some reason, which would later become obvious, they wouldn't. When Diamonds' two sisters came home, both gems in their own right, and then Papa Diamonds, a doctor with a heart of gold and generosity to match, the picture was complete. After a small meal hastily got together the parents went out and Chet sat and read Ginsberg's *Howl* at the youngest daughter's request (she was studying it and having problems relating) while I accompanied him on the piano. Kevin laughed at the drug references. Later when the parents returned, Chet and I, worried that the house might be full for Thanksgiving, offered to leave and find a motel. But they wouldn't hear of it and we had a bed for the night as well as an invite to Thanksgiving lunch the next day at friends. Before we hit the sack however Kevin began to show his true colours, and not able to handle the fact that we were staying and he wasn't, began shouting at Diamonds upstairs in her bedroom.

If I leave you're going to sleep with them aren't you?

During the evening, the daughter studying literature asked me about theatre in London. I told her I'd seen Anthony Hopkins play King Lear at the National. Kevin then came into the kitchen and hearing me pronounce the production as excellent, started to shout Excellent! at the top of his voice. As Wayne's World had yet to hit England, I didn't get the joke and he mistook my ignorance as rudeness. He then grabbed a carving knife and ran into the garden.

This had been coming.

All through dinner, as we all chatted away in a convivial manner, Kevin would suddenly turn to me and ask, Why are you doing this? I looked round to see if anyone else had heard but no-one seemed to. While I was playing piano I could feel his stare piercing into my neck. And then in the kitchen with the excellent King Lear slip, Kevin grabs the carving knife and runs out into the snow.

What's he doing here? Why do this? Who are they gonna fuck? Who the fuck fucks those fucking fucks?

He didn't come in and kill us all but ran off into the moonlight as Papa Diamonds had predicted. Papa was in bed and wasn't going to stir. The sisters sat huddled together until we were sure and then we all retired. Chet and I fell asleep still laughing about it.

Thanksgiving was a revelation. The two hostesses worked as caterers so the food kept coming. And before this, the three daughters came down in their Sunday best and wow! Was this a sight. Chet fell heavily for the middle daughter and eulogised her the whole trip back. Before the meal we held hands and sang 'Kumbaya' – which made me feel uncomfortable, but looking round I was surprised to see everyone singing and seeming to mean it. We drove back from Thanksgiving in two cars. Myself, Diamonds and her mother in one. Papa Diamonds, the other daughters and Chet in the other. In my car I repeated the story of how we drove from Ohio to Minneapolis without an address, and then in front of mother and daughter, claimed to find the house through pure feeling. Maybe it was the food and wine but I got a bit carried away and erased the part about the kind neighbour giving us the number.

I could tell it was your house as we drove past.

How? Asked the mother.

I don't know. I could just feel it.

Diamonds had tears in her eyes and so did her mother.

It's funny how you look back and realise one lie ruins everything.

Back in England my gran had to sell her flat so I moved to London and spent a lot of time in Archway Towers, home of the housing benefit unit of the Department of Social Security. If Kafka had ever written a novel called The Tower he would have set it here. My Greek landlord, Mister D, would come round on the first of every month and expect his rent. Out of a house of six rooms with anything up to ten people living in he usually got about four rents. The two who usually couldn't pay were myself and John, a musician. Mister D liked us two though and let us decide who stayed there; this privilege overtaken by the desperate need to cover at least some of the rent. We let anybody in. John had quit/got sacked from his chauffeuring work and so his claim had to got through appeal (add another month to the three we'd been waiting). The trick with these cheques is to make sure you've somewhere to move when they come through and use your momentary richness as collateral. After reaching the relevant floor of Archway Towers you take a ticket, similar to the ones you get in butcher's shops. There were close to a hundred people in each of the three sections to get through before you were finished. I was first level, making an enquiry, hassling for a date to tell my hovering landlord. To give you an idea of how long it took my number to come round: I'd taken a Russian novel with me, and managed to read one hundred and forty-seven pages before being called. Single men, bottom of the pile in terms of preference, had to wait so long they'd fall asleep, and if you miss your number being called; that was it. Join the end of the queue. Take another ticket. Some of them would talk as if they were professional Archway Towerers, who queued to be let in, got passed from one counter to the next, until the impossible-to-fill-in forms were correct. Then they'd prologise about the surreal leap in floors. From enquiries to confirmations.

This floor was even worse. The din, smoke and shouting hit fever pitch. Everyone was so geared up to being so close to floor three they could hardly contain themselves. Nirvana was in sight. I got to the third floor once, five months later, when after they lost my forms not once but twice, I finally saw hard cash. I once asked if there was a way of speeding up the process. Get yourself an eviction order from the landlord, they said, you'll get your money in two weeks then! The payment floor was the empty one. In the two hours I sat, waiting for the cheque to be stamped, I saw one other person who had to be directed back downstairs. Wrong floor mate! How I pitied him as he smiled and walked back into the throng.

Of all the people who came and went in the months I spent in that house, John's friend David was the only real character. David was a rockabilly from New Zealand. He had the sharp suits and perfect quiff and even a tattoo of British Rocker on his chest. I asked how as a Kiwi, he felt entitled to wear it, and he took my mild rebuke as a personal slight and this set the tone for the love/hate months to come. David was trying to put his life's dream into operation, a club called The Arches in Camden. He'd rented an old railway arch from British Rail and was busy single-handedly re-building it. He wanted to be ready for an impossible deadline. David got us all to work on the club one day but bemused by us not wanting to stay after dark, dismissed us with a wave of the hand.

No-one's getting anything out of the club who doesn't help build it now!

It was going to be open or kill him. And it was killing him. Every night he came in, a feverish look in his eye, his perfect dancer's frame exhausted from a day drilling, painting, loading, carrying, installing. Then he'd go round up anybody in the house who wanted to go out partying. I was the only one up for these trips.

We'd start at the Green Lanes Football Club bars; focal points for the Cypriot community. Here we'd be the only English speakers in a pool hall of middle-aged men and the odd teenager. You never saw women. David would buy beer, expensive and disgusting, and we'd play pool. Then we'd have a full meal in one of the local restaurants with kebab, bread, wine, yoghurt, Irish coffee. He'd rail against me as an idealist, a romantic and I enjoyed his antagonism. His rages only really came into the house when one of the newcomers would dismantle his beloved shower curtain. David never warned them about the precariousness of this item and neither did I. In they'd come, fancy a bath instead of a shower and down it went. David would get up, spend hours on the phone trying to organise some help at The Arches (a constant failure) – then towel round waist he'd head for the bathroom. Seeing the curtain, which was no more than some black bin liners attached to a pole, on the floor, David would then go into a shouting and screaming fit that would last near on twenty minutes. I timed him once. Many of the people who left did so because of these rages, although he never laid a finger on anyone.

One night we were on Holloway Road, close to where the down and outs slept. To my amazement, David seemed to know everyone and began handing out beers and twenty-pound notes. One night he was standing in the hallway drunk, shaking and so upset/high over something he actually pissed his pants. John and I stood there. Neither of us looked away. John had fallen out with him over the phone bill and during their arguing David had threatened to break his fingers. A particularly nasty threat to lay on a guitarist.

On my last night I went out with him again. We went to the Queens Head, Turnpike Lane. A bikers' pub. David looked fine in his fifties suit but I was seriously out of place with my cropped hair and trainers. We began to play pool in

our usual confrontational style and it started to piss him off
how many games I was winning.

What do you want me to do man, lose?

One of the bikers came over and told us to keep it down.
We sat back at the bar.

You're so lucky you are, Slim. So lucky.

It's not luck. I'm a natural at all sports.

What about dancing?

That's not a sport.

Okay arm wrestling.

I know I should have declined but I thought he'd win. He
was all pumped up from a day's exertion at The Arches and I
felt flabby through bad eating. I put my arm down half-heartedly, expecting it to be over in a flash and then I'd buy him a
drink. But it never works that way. Feeling the downward
pressure halfway to the table, my pride fought back. Soon I
was level. Then I won. Hell's Angels were hovering. David
could hardly look at me as they threw us out.

Halfway home, he suddenly turned to me and said,
Watch this.

He crossed Green Lanes to an arcade and challenged the
first two guys he could to fight me. They were two Latinos,
dressed in hip hop gear, and looked like the kind of guys who
didn't take any shit in their lives. The meaner-looking of the
two said,
Fine, I'll take him on.

But I'd seen enough. Crossing the road, I walked away.
Left him to it.

Flashback 1

I was having dinner with this girl. Cheap Italian place. Flowers on the wall. And in the course of her recounting this long, involved story, she caught me looking at myself in the mirrored glass above the table. With great delight she confronted me but I remained non-plussed. I didn't blush nor bother to deny it.

Yes I often do that, I said and returned to the food.

She ended our relationship with a telephone call. This was cold, brutal. But it summed up what we had. She said,

I bet you don't even know the colour of my eyes, do you?

Yes, I do, I said, lying compulsively: but I couldn't think of them. Hazel? Black?

What are they then? What colour? She persisted.

Flashback 2

Louis and I both hit perfect tee shots. My brother stepped up, addressed his ball and hit it straight into the trees. As was customary with Jack, he then used all his strength to launch his golf club in the direction of the ball. He must have slipped. The club did a weird spin in the air and caught Louis full in the face. It was a fairly hefty blow, and must have hurt, but Louis followed my lead in these things and laughed it off. It was an accident, Jack was very sorry, he hadn't meant to do it. The only thing broken was a lens in Louis' glasses, needed replacing anyway...

At that moment, bending down to pick up his spectacles, Louis experienced a childhood flashback that rooted him to the spot.

'I was sat up in bed, listening to my parents shouting, scared. I remember walking across the hallway and lowering myself to sit on the top stair. It was then it went off. Two or three things consecutively. I sat, something broke downstairs, a shriek, and then – as if in slow motion because I watched it all the way – a slither of glass flew through the air and into my eye. It was like a bullet, you could see it coming – just – but you had no time to move. I felt no pain as it entered but I wanted to cry out in shock. I muffled the sound with my hand as I was terrified my parents would catch me eavesdropping.

'There was no blood from the injury, nothing I could find in the eye; the glass had simply gone in and disappeared. Did

I imagine it, who knows? What I am sure of, from that night forward, my eyesight began to deteriorate. It wasn't long before I needed glasses just to walk down the street.'

Flashback 3

In the hot afternoons, Jack and I would walk down to the campsite and join in the five-a-sides. That day we were losing 2-1 to the French, final whistle pending, I played my brother in; an inch-perfect pass to the wing. Jack rounded his defender, made it to the byline, was about to pull it back to me steaming into the centre, when… He slipped. Dust rose from the loose gravel, the ball span harmlessly behind. Whistle blows. Game over.

You dick! I shout, enjoying his misfortune, a football moment; the one sport at which Jack excelled over me. Then I heard the crack. The sharp unmistakable gut-wrenching crack of human bone. My brother, continuing his run after failing to deliver the telling cross, ran straight over to a concrete ledge and kicked his ankle against it, in temper, with all his might. My father, who was also playing, the French; all thought he had kicked the ledge accidentally.

Growing up, we'd fight each other with cues in the snooker room. Eventually my father refused to replace them. My brother kneeling on the floor, head-butting the ground until he knocked himself out. Was he happy then? Just because he lost. At tennis, he had an unfortunate habit of hitting backhands into the net. To win, I only had to serve that side. His punishment for this was to pound his wrist on the tarmac until tears streamed down his face. I've often wondered what his best friend Louis made of these outbursts. That tennis afternoon we'd been playing doubles, our cousins leaving in disgust at the bad language and lack of sportmanship, but I had match point on my second serve. I looped it up high, knowing my brother hated to look up into the sun and aimed the ball well wide, so he had no choice but to attempt a backhand return. Smack, the ball hit the top of the net, flopped back his side. Game, set and… My brother is on his knees, pounding and pounding his wrist on the hard court. After the first two blows, he looks at his wrist, looks at me and asks,

Why won't it break?

Flashback 4

Two days on and the love/hate thing continues... How to fight? It was like the time you were walking on the beach Chet, and you fell and I asked, How do you feel? Do you remember?

How do you feel?

And you said, I fell, feeling the same way now. I fell, feeling the same way now. I couldn't understand it but it stayed in my mind. It has stayed. Right up till now. Up till today. But now what? Now what do you feel?

Do you remember that girl you saw in that bar that time? That girl. And you asked me to describe her and I said, Red hair and a husky voice just to see if you'd react to a cliché. You know? See if I could jolt you. And do you remember how you kept on about how weird it was to say something about the timbre of her voice when what was required was a physical description? Obviously, you added. And how someone's voice might have counted if it had been a telephone conversation or a gig, but not some bar scene. Not some girl in a bar.

Flashback 5

The black man standing on the balcony of the Hotel Splendide in Nice. His arms outstretched. An everyday noir crucifix to the midday sun. For me his eyebeam seeming to bounce on water. The locals claimed he always wore a white blouse so that his sleeves appeared imaginary. I asked him once if his arms ever got tired.

An injury to the inner arm, he stated, should only be bandaged with imaginary sleeves.

Road Trip

Louis was then living with his girlfriend in Forest Hill. We arranged to meet at his place for dinner. When I arrived Louis said there was no food in the house, so we defrosted a pack of bagels in the microwave and sat there eating them. Louis and his girlfriend had been having relationship problems, and as the evening wore on he filled me in on recent developments. But behind all this there was something nagging away. Eventually I dragged it out of him. Louis had become obsessed with a girl he'd seen for five minutes at a party. He didn't know where she lived, but remembered overhearing her talk about a mews near Victoria Station with an elegant balcony. At the party the girl had been describing the horrendous grief she'd had getting her piano in. For some reason this clinched it for me. I said to Louis,

Shall we go and look for her then?

I knew we'd do this tonight, he said. And out we went.

As with all our road trips in search of women, the smaller the clues, the sharper the enthusiasm. No music this time, just the sound of the engine, the wheels spinning in the direction of Victoria Station. We both waited for the flow without mentioning it. The flow being our name for what a non-believer would call a rush of adrenalin or an esoteric Buddhist might describe as ordinary mind/highest mind. First of all we headed to the west side, in that second not knowing why, it just seemed like the right side. I, as usual, in the passenger seat, began the interrogation. What was she

like, would she live alone, did she have a car, would she leave
it outside? Yes. The car was the first clue. He remembered
seeing her drive away in an orange hatchback. So around the
west side we went, searching for an orange car parked
outside a balconied mews. West side, we realised, more likely
for a mews. All the time I'm pressing Louis for details, trying
to feed his obsession. The flow was raggedy at first. We found
a car which looked like hers but the street it was parked in
was dwarfed by Victorian monstrosities; rising up like halls
of residence and blocking our light. The car in question, right
kind, right colour, just wrong choice of cassettes. It was full of
Christian worship tapes, Clifford Hill etc and Louis felt this
was wrong. He had a hunch she wasn't a Christian. We got
back in the car, headed south. We'd been looking for about an
hour now, one miss only served to heighten our intensity. I
opened my window a little, it was becoming hard to breathe.
Two men in close proximity, trying to will a meeting, a face in
a window. I'm trying to keep names out of it, but names are
important. We kept repeating hers, trance-like with a little
giggle after. The car racing up and down streets, through traffic lights, past cornershops, pubs, the odd skateboarder,
women alone. We wanted one woman now, no decisions
made yet as to whether Louis would approach should we
find her. It is all now, now, now. She, she, she. We came to a
crossroads, we actually went past the road. Louis hadn't
really looked, hadn't turned his neck, it was my side; I should
have seen it but I hadn't. It was his obsession after all, he felt
it as we passed. We were stationary then at the traffic lights,
we'd been up and through them twice already, it was getting
near ten o'clock. I remember checking. Louis suddenly
screeched the car around as the lights changed, did a U-turn
and back we went, back to the last road on the left before the
traffic lights. Last road on the left before the traffic lights. I
repeated the mantra. Louis insisted he get out alone and go
visit. This wasn't in fact her road but it led to it. A mews road
which split at the bottom. A T-junction. Which way? He
chose right, don't ask me how, we turned a blind corner and

there it was. The orange hatchback, the mews cottage, the ivy-laden balcony. Louis cut off the engine. We were both worked up now, sweat pouring from our brows. Eyes glued together, his gaze was too fierce for me, I looked away. Louis was leaning forward, staring at the car, at her house.

Are you gonna go then?

I'm thinking of what to do, he explained.

Louis had a lot at stake. What about his girlfriend? He lived with her. Should he cross the line and approach the house? I knew in my heart of hearts there was no choice, but Louis, a calm and rational person outside the flow, knew what he was and what he had to lose. Was he going to throw it all away on a girl he saw once? I thought if he leaves the car all will be lost. He leaves the car... I, talking like the clappers, trying to get him to let me come too. And he, it took over ten minutes of persuasion, with me going; what difference does it make now? Just for me to see her? Let me see her and I'll go back to the car. I won't come in. With neither of us considering she was out, Louis rang the doorbell. Her father came to the window and asked what we wanted. Louis said her name and we were informed she was staying with a friend. The father's voice sound harsh, brusque. He was in a silk dressing gown and had a woman waiting. I heard a laugh...

Back to the car. Louis and I drove away in total silence. What did this mean? Was the flow broken? No, we'd found where she lived. The object of tonight's drive. To see her, for her to be in and for Louis to go in and rave at her like an insane person, surely this was what the flow was protecting him from? Now he had a choice, did he want to see her or not? Was it just a passing fancy brought on by problems at home or more serious? Could he stand to go home tonight without seeing her? And lastly, the question I didn't dare voice, what would happen when he went home and faced his girlfriend? I knew Louis would tell her everything later. We all had this strange rule where our women were concerned: as long as they knew about it, it was fine. Louis answered all questions by writing the girl a note. He wrote, in pencil, on the back of a work sheet, and then sat, dead still, and read it to me. I wish I had a duplicate. It was a classic. Hysterical in its attempt to be casual: laughable in its effort to shrug the whole evening off as one of those things. The first two lines were,

I don't know what's happened, but there's some connection between us, do you feel it? If so -

And then he left his phone number and signed his name. I was laughing at the note, laughing at the entire enterprise, but not laughing in any safe affordable way, it was like the laugh of a murderer who had just been sentenced.

Louis dropped me home about two in the morning; he had yet to face his girlfriend, tell her, get up and go to work the next morning. It was excruciating not to be able to witness those scenes, and I fully expected a phone call the next day to say he was out on his ear, bags packed, everything. But I didn't hear from him for three months and when I did he didn't mention that night. Eventually, six months later, in preparation for what would become our last road trip together, I asked him if there had been any fallout from the night. He said,

More than you can ever imagine.

The Last Road Trip

W hy blow on a flame which has already died? What do you remember above all from the trip? Wales, Cornwall, the rocks, Merlin's Cave, Louis head-over-heels in the water twice, the green slime he slipped on, the water coming in and him disappearing, me standing there, trying to make a decision, trying to read what I was feeling, trying to stop laughing. Why did no-one (we) take his injury seriously at the hospital?

We left London mid-afternoon and got down to Wales as it was getting dark. We were searching for King Arthur's stone; the one he pulled the sword from. It didn't actually exist according to the guide book I had on my lap, but there was a cove and castle where it was last seen, which on the full moon apparently, the ghost of a soldier in full armour could be seen wading out to sea. This was good enough for us and to the coast we headed. The Gower Peninsula runs right across one whole flank of Welsh coastline and we edged our way down it. The sea roaring; we squinted out. It was when we passed through a village called Three Crosses that I felt the flow begin to activate. Calvary symbolism being too strong to ignore, we turned round. The wind was now howling across deserted stretches of marshland: one pub, some cottages but not a cross to be seen. I wasn't expecting to see any, but the kind of mood I get myself in on these trips encourages willed images. Stopping in the pub for a pint and a pie, I remembered the Eubank fight was on and all the villagers were huddled in there, mostly old folk, sitting round wooden tables, staring up at the screen. I asked the barman about a castle on a cove, and he said,

You mean the National Trust place, overlooking the sea?

Trying to contain my excitement I nodded and listened to the instructions he gave. We were only a five-minute drive away. Louis and I finished our drinks. Eubank was on the ropes when we left but I knew he wasn't the one in trouble. Back at the car the wind and rain were bucketing down, we had to use fog lights to see; straining every five yards to negotiate the weaving lanes we drove down. It was then we saw it. A smoky silhouette in the distance, a crumbling facade. A castle, the cove, the moon behind. The locked gate. It was now eleven. For some reason I tried the gate anyway and sure enough it opened to touch. We drove in. There was a house in the distance with lights on. Landlord's place, I concluded, dogs barking, turn the engine off, move forward without light. We got out of the car. First thing I remember, after dodging the sheepdog, was the touch of rock. The castle wall so hard and defined to the finger, after such devastation from afar. I was trying to get to grips with this as we walked round and the view out to sea hit us. We had no room for it. Back off. Back wall propped up by boulders, grass verges cut away; sweeping down to marshland. Beyond the marsh, strange circles of light on the horizon. They could have been cut grass, irrigation ditches, but they had a different tone to the blackness all around. Black, but back-lit by moonlight. Why did we try and get down the hill? It was so dangerous, a sheer drop, to what? You couldn't see the bottom. We clung to each other as the slide started. I can't remember who fell first. The fall was brief; gorse bushes stopping us. Standing up, pricked a bit, but laughing, I was determined to know what the circles of light meant. All of a sudden, at this level there were no longer three circles but one. We stopped. The one circle: we had gorged ourselves on Arthurian legend all the way down to get in the mood for a quest, I reading the guide book cover to cover. I turned to Louis, an insane glint in my eye.

You know the circle?

Don't tell me, he says, The Round Table?

Needless to say a cynic with us would have laughed out loud, but we continued. Hitting the bottom level when our sightlines should have been level with it, the circle disappeared. We wandered through the mud but there was nothing. What did it mean? Corn circles in a marsh? Don't think so. It was then I looked up at the moon. Saw a cloud. I turned to Louis and whispered,

Look I know this is complete lunacy, but is that cloud shaped like a sword coming out of a stone, or what?

Louis couldn't take his eyes off it.

If you wanted to see it like that you could, he said, curiously neither confirming nor denying. Whatever it was we got the flow back and felt strong enough to try and climb the hill. At the top we heard dogs. More than one. And they were loose.

What do we do?

Go back down.

Again the tumble, again the gorse, again neither of us hurt. There was a public footpath back but we had to walk the perimeter of the marsh to make it. It took a while. Where was the car? I started to lose it, going on about the armies of the night attacking this hill in years gone by and we both played off each other until we were hysterical. I looked over at him. He was white.

I can see their auras, he was shouting, Quick!

Where was the car? We got to the gate, closed it as the dogs came, opened the car doors, got in, locked them. Louis turned the ignition and we were gone. He said,

Maybe we imagined the dogs, in the same way we imagined the circle of light, the soldiers. Maybe we never actually left the car?

He drove straight through the night to Cornwall. Who could do such a thing: get straight back in, turn the key and away? It was not possible. Louis said there was no way he was staying the night in Three Crosses. I nodded. We sipped at the flask of whisky, passing it back and forth. I can see Louis leant at the wheel, tapes we played, rotated. I don't recall any of the driving, the roads. I never saw any coastline. I woke up and we were at Tintagel.

Cornwall. 5am. We tried to sleep for a few hours, reclined in our seats, in sleeping bags. As the light began to rise I looked out at Tintagel in the new light of morning. The castle set in the rock, magnificent. I attempted to contrast it with the wreck of the Three Crosses castle, make that real. We had to wait two hours for it to be open for the public. We had breakfast in a café where the woman charged more if you had two slices of toast with your scrambled egg rather than one. Louis considered this fair enough but I've always hated meanness and raged against her all the way out. Little things like that can spoil whole trips for me. On our way round the sea wall to the castle we got sidetracked by Merlin's Cave. The guide book said it was where he stayed when visiting King Arthur. Coachloads of tourists began to arrive.

Forget the castle, I said, the cave's what we've come for. The stone will be in there. Trust me.

The cave has no real access point, one shaky path which winds its way round the cliff face. From there you have to triple jump across three rocks to reach Merlin's Cave. The sea was high that day, the wind lashing. None of the American/Japanese tourists who joined us would take the risk. The sign said,

If you go further than this point you are in grave danger.

It didn't read to me like a National Trust sign so I ignored it. Anyway I like the word: grave. It's like the word: insane. As long as you're going in to something, you're fine. Louis and I left the tourists behind. We made it round the rocks, gingerly stepping onto the last dry section. I could smell the salt. We saw the three stones. Both of us counted the seconds before the waves came in and flooded them. About five seconds, we agreed. Plenty of time as long as you didn't pause. You've got to do it all in one motion. Hop, skip and jump. One two three. No four, five. Then the water came. A huge tube of it, crashing against the face. We concentrated. There was no talk of turning round. Tourists were filming us with their videos. I knelt down on the cold rock, put my hand in the water and felt my flesh freeze. I washed my face, enjoyed getting the sleep out of my eyes and replacing it with stinging salt. I tried blinking to clear. The blur went. I was kneeling now, almost praying with concentration. Get the tourists out of your mind, I was thinking. This is not a show. This is important. This means something. What? I stood up. I was ready. I was going to go jump when…

Louis launched himself towards the first rock. He made it. I was willing him on, counting the seconds, checking the water, fully expecting him to spring on to the second rock in the same movement; he did… it was here the problems started. He hesitated on the second rock. What happened? Did he panic, lose it, think about the water? All I know is the water came in and he went flying. Head over heels, literally, an amazing somersault from a standing position, lifted up by the water; his head missing the main cliff section by inches. He was swimming for a second, then standing as the water went out again. I was helpless with laughter. Why? Friends have said I lack compassion. They're probably right. But I still felt for him. I wasn't laughing at him. Just at the whole pathetic got to pay for two fucking pieces of toast with your scrambled egg mentality! If that woman could see us now, would she still charge us? She'd probably ban us. Still, you worry about how much bread to give customers, love, and I'll get my friend out of the water! Louis knew he had another five seconds to get back on the second rock and either jump back or keep going to the cave. He tried to come back, but instead of standing on the second rock, hopping onto the first and clear, he panicked and tried to climb along the seaweed on the cliff wall. Sure enough he slipped and it was then I heard the horrific crack after the tide came in. It swept him under. I wasn't laughing now. At first I thought he had broken his neck. He was thrown like a rag doll. He resurfaced, spitting and clawing at the rock, the water subsiding.

Another five seconds. This time he made it. All the while I just stood there. I did nothing. I helped him to the shore, made a gangway as the tourists crowded round. Again I was laughing: in shock? Louis lifted up the middle finger on his right hand, first of all. It was bent at right angles, huge, swollen. He had a change of clothes in the back of the car, and as he stripped I saw the battering his body had taken. I was now driving, still laughing, but driving. It took hours to find a hospital. We were in the middle of nowhere. When we arrived they X-rayed the finger and said it was smashed to smithereens. Every tiny bone in it was broken. It was irreparable. Crippled for life. We drove home in complete silence.

Back in London I left before his girlfriend got home from work. I sat on the tube shellshocked. Louis couldn't stop shivering, even with three blankets round him. Something had come to an end, we both knew, and as I exited at my stop, I asked myself, Does this mean something? Is it important that someone got hurt?

BLOODLINES the cutting-edge crime and mystery imprint...

That Angel Look by Mike Ripley

"The outrageous, rip-roarious Mr Ripley is an abiding delight..."
– Colin Dexter

A chance encounter (in a pub, of course) lands street-wise, cab-driving Angel the ideal job as an all-purpose assistant to a trio of young and very sexy fashion designers.

But things are nowhere near as straightforward as they should be and it soon becomes apparent that no-one is telling the truth – least of all Angel! 1 899344 23 3 – £8

Fresh Blood II edited by Mike Ripley & Maxim Jakubowski

Follow-up to the highly-acclaimed original volume (see below), featuring short stories from John Baker, Christopher Brookmyre, Ken Bruen, Carol Anne Davis, Christine Green, Lauren Henderson, Charles Higson, Maxim Jakubowski, Phil Lovesey, Mike Ripley, Iain Sinclair, John Tilsley, John Williams, and RD Wingfield (Inspector Frost)
ISBN 1 899 344 20 9 – £8.

Fresh Blood edited by Mike Ripley & Maxim Jakubowski

Featuring the cream of the British New Wave of crime writers including John Harvey, Mark Timlin, Chaz Brenchley, Russell James, Stella Duffy, Ian Rankin, Nicholas Blincoe, Joe Canzius, Denise Danks, John B Spencer, Graeme Gordon, and a previously unpublished extract from the late Derek Raymond. Includes an introduction from each author explaining their views on crime fiction in the '90s and a comprehensive foreword on the genre from Angel-creator, Mike Ripley.
ISBN 1 899344 03 9 – £6.99

BLOODLINES the cutting-edge crime and mystery imprint...

JOHN B SPENCER

Tooth & Nail by John B Spencer

The long-awaited new noir thriller from the author of *Perhaps She'll Die*. A dark, Rackmanesque tale of avarice and malice-afore-thought from one of Britain's most exciting and accomplished writers. "Spencer offers yet another demonstration that our crime writers can hold their own with the best of their American counter-parts when it comes to snappy dialogue and criminal energy. Recommended." – *Time Out*
ISBN 1 899344 31 4 – £7

Perhaps She'll Die! by John B Spencer

Giles could never say 'no' to a woman... any woman. But when he tangled with Celeste, he made a mistake... A bad mistake.

Celeste was married to Harry, and Harry walked a dark side of the street that Giles – with his comfortable lifestyle and fashionable media job – could only imagine in his worst nightmares. And when Harry got involved in nightmares, people had a habit of getting hurt. Set against the boom and gloom of eighties Britain, *Perhaps She'll Die!* is classic *noir* with a centre as hard as toughened diamond.
ISBN 1 899344 14 4 – £5.99

Quake City by John B Spencer

The third novel to feature Charley Case, the hard-boiled investiga-tor of a future that follows the 'Big One of Ninety-Seven' – the quake that literally rips California apart and makes LA an Island.

"Classic Chandleresque private eye tale, jazzed up by being set in the future... but some things never change – PI Charley Case still has trouble with women and a trusty bottle of bourbon is always at hand. An entertaining addition to the private eye canon." – *Mail on Sunday*
ISBN 1 899344 02 0 – £5.99

BLOODLINES the cutting-edge crime and mystery imprint...

Smalltime by Jerry Raine

Smalltime is a taut, psychological crime thriller, set among the seedy world of petty criminals and no-hopers. In this remarkable début, Jerry Raine shows just how easily curiosity can turn into fear amid the horrors, despair and despondency of life lived a little too near the edge.

"Jerry Raine's *Smalltime* carries the authentic whiff of sleazy nineties Britain. He vividly captures the world of stunted ambitions and their evil consequences." – Simon Brett

"The first British contemporary crime novel featuring an underclass which no one wants. Absolutely authentic and quite possibly important."– Philip Oakes, *Literary Review*.

ISBN 1 899344 13 6 – £5.99

Hellbent on Homicide by Gary Lovisi

"This isn't a first novel, this is a book written by a craftsman who learned his business from the masters, and in HELLBENT ON HOMICIDE, that education rings loud and long." –Eugene Izzi

1962, a sweet, innocent time in America... after McCarthy, before Vietnam. A time of peace and trust, when girls hitch-hiked without a care. But for an ice-hearted killer, a time of easy pickings.

"A wonderful throwback to the glory days of hardboiled American crime fiction. In my considered literary judgement, if you pass up HELLBENT ON HOMICIDE, you're a stone chump." –Andrew Vachss

Brooklyn-based Gary Lovisi's powerhouse début novel is a major contribution to the hardboiled school, a roller-coaster of sex, violence and suspense, evocative of past masters like Jim Thompson, Carroll John Daly and Ross Macdonald.

"A sharp pistol crack of a book, pure and loving homage to the hard-boiled pulps of yesteryear." – *The Daily Telegraph*

ISBN 1 899344 18 7 £7

BLOODLINES the cutting-edge crime and mystery imprint…

The Hackman Blues by Ken Bruen

"If Martin Amis was writing crime novels, this is what he would hope to write." – *Books in Ireland*

"…I haven't taken my medication for the past week. If I couldn't go a few days without the lithium, I was in deep shit. I'd gotten the job ten days earlier and it entailed a whack of pub-crawling. Booze and medication is the worst of songs. Sing that!

A job of pure simplicity. Find a white girl in Brixton. Piece of cake. What I should have done is doubled my medication and lit a candle to St Jude – maybe a lot of candles."

Add to the mixture a lethal ex-con, an Irish builder obsessed with Gene Hackman, the biggest funeral Brixton has ever seen, and what you get is the Blues like they've never been sung before.

Ken Bruen's powerful second novel is a gritty and grainy mix of crime noir and Urban Blues that greets you like a mugger stays with you like a razor-scar.

GQ described his début novel as:

"The most startling and original crime novel of the decade."

The Hackman Blues is Ken Bruen's best novel yet.

ISBN 1899344 22 5 – £7

Shrouded by Carol Anne Davis

Douglas likes women — quiet women; the kind he deals with at the mortuary where he works. Douglas meets Marjorie, unemployed, gaining weight and losing confidence. She talks and laughs a lot to cover up her shyness, but what Douglas really needs is a lover who'll stay still — deadly still. Driven by lust and fear, Douglas finds a way to make girls remain excitingly silent and inert. But then he is forced to blank out the details of their unplanned deaths.

Perhaps only Marjorie can fulfil his growing sexual hunger. If he could just get her into a state of limbo. Douglas studies his textbooks to find a way…

Shrouded is a powerful and accomplished début, tautly-plotted, dangerously erotic and vibrating with tension and suspense.

ISBN 1 899344 17 9— £7

BLOODLINES the cutting-edge crime and mystery imprint...

PAUL CHARLES

Last Boat To Camden Town by Paul Charles

The second enthralling Detective Inspector Christy Kennedy mystery. The body of Dr Edmund Godfrey Berry is discovered at the bottom of the Regent's Canal, in the heart of Kennedy's "patch" of Camden Town, north London. But the question is, Did he jump, or was he pushed? Last Boat to Camden Town combines Whodunnit? Howdunnit? and love story with Paul Charles' trademark unique-method-of-murder to produce one of the best detective stories of the year.

"If you enjoy Morse, you'll enjoy Kennedy" – Talking Music, BBC Radio 2

Hardback: ISBN 1 899344 29 2 – £15

Paperback: ISBN 1 899344 30 6 – £7

I Love The Sound of Breaking Glass by Paul Charles

First outing for Irish-born Detective Inspector Christy Kennedy whose beat is Camden Town, north London. Peter O'Browne, managing director of Camden Town Records, is missing. Is his disappearance connected with a mysterious fire that ravages his north London home? And just who was using his credit card in darkest Dorset?

Although up to his neck in other cases, Detective Inspector Christy Kennedy and his team investigate, plumbing the hidden depths of London's music industry, turning up murder, chart-rigging scams, blackmail and worse. *I Love The Sound of Breaking Glass* is a detective story with a difference. Part whodunnit, part howdunnit and part love story, it features a unique method of murder, a plot with more twists and turns than the road from Kingsmarkham to St Mary Mead.

Paul Charles is one of Europe's best known music promoters and agents. In this, his stunning début, he reveals himself as master of the crime novel.

ISBN 1 899344 16 0 – £7

It's Not A Runner Bean by Mark Steel

'I've never liked Mark Steel and I thoroughly resent the high quality of this book.' – Jack Dee

The life of a Slightly Successful Comedian can include a night spent on bare floorboards next to a pyromaniac squatter in Newcastle, followed by a day in Chichester with someone so aristocratic, they speak without ever moving their lips.

From his standpoint behind the microphone, Mark Steel is in the perfect position to view all human existence. Which is why this book – like his act, broadcasts and series' – is opinionated, passionate, and extremely funny. It even gets around to explaining the line (screamed at him by an Eighties yuppy): 'It's not a runner bean...' – which is another story.

'Hugely funny...' – *Time Out*

'A terrific book. I have never read any other book about comedy written by someone with a sense of humour.' – Jeremy Hardy, *Socialist Review*.

ISBN 1 899344 12 8– £5.99

The Strange Adventures of the Dangerous Sports Club by Martin Lyster

This is the inside true story of an informal group of amateur adventurers (including soldiers, academics, an MP and a member of the Monty Python team) who broke laws, legs and chandeliers around the world, leaving a trail of crashed cars, unpaid bills, empty bottles and overturned conventions in their wake. Fully illustrated.

"Martin Lyster's *The Strange Adventures of the Dangerous Sports Club* is a must. Utterly fascinating." – *Time Out*

ISBN 1 899344 28 4.– £8

Will You Hold Me? by Christopher Kenworthy

Christopher Kenworthy's intense, mood-laden stories expertly explore the vulnerable under-belly of human emotion. From the sleazy backstreets of Paris to huddled London bedrooms, his characters inhabit a world where hope too often turns to despair and where compassion is rewarded with malice. Christopher Kenworthy is a writer at the cutting edge of contemporary fiction, and this is the first collection of his brilliantly original stories.

"The voice is original, plain, pained. The content borders on the gothic. The effect is to reveal both magic and menace as being present in the ordinary." — Geoff Ryman, author of *Was*

ISBN 1 899344 11 X — £6.99

Elvis – The Novel by Robert Graham, Keith Baty

'Quite simply, the greatest music book ever written'
        – Mick Mercer, *Melody Maker*

The everyday tale of an imaginary superstar eccentric. The Presley neither his fans nor anyone else knew. First-born of triplets, he came from the backwoods of Tennessee. Driven by a burning ambition to sing opera, Fate sidetracked him into creating Rock 'n' roll.

His classic movie, *Driving A Sportscar Down To A Beach In Hawaii* didn't win the Oscar he yearned for, but The Beatles revived his flagging spirits, and he stunned the world with a guest appearance in Batman.

Further shockingly momentous events have led him to the peaceful, contented lifestyle he enjoys today.

'Books like this are few and far between.' – Charles Shaar Murray, *NME*

ISBN 1 899344 19 5 – £7

The Users by Brian Case

The welcome return of Brian Case's brilliantly original '60s cult classic.

'A remarkable debut' –Anthony Burgess

'Why Case's spiky first novel from 1968 should have languished for nearly thirty years without a reprint must be one of the enigmas of modern publishing. Mercilessly funny and swaggeringly self-conscious, it could almost be a template for an early Martin Amis.'
– *Sunday Times.*

ISBN 1 899344 05 5 – £5.99

Charlie's Choice: The First Charlie Muffin Omnibus by Brian Freemantle – *Charlie Muffin; Clap Hands, Here Comes Charlie; The Inscrutable Charlie Muffin*

Charlie Muffin is not everybody's idea of the ideal espionage agent. Dishevelled, cantankerous and disrespectful, he refuses to play by the Establishment's rules. Charlie's axiom is to screw anyone from anywhere to avoid it happening to him. But it's not long before he finds himself offered up as an unwilling sacrifice by a disgraced Department, desperate to win points in a ruthless Cold War. Now for the first time, the first three Charlie Muffin books are collected together in one volume.

'Charlie is a marvellous creation' – *Daily Mail*

ISBN 1 899344 26 8 – £9

Also available in paperback from The Do-Not Press

MILES GIBSON

Dancing With Mermaids by Miles Gibson

'Absolutely first rate. Absolutely wonderful' – Ray Bradbury
Strange things are afoot in the Dorset fishing town of Rams Horn.
Set close to the poisonous swamps at the mouth of the River
Sheep, the town has been isolated from its neighbours for cen-
turies. But mysterious events are unfolding... A seer who has
waited for years for her drowned husband to reappear is haunted
by demons, an African sailor arrives from the sea and takes refuge
with a widow and her idiot daughter. Young boys plot sexual
crimes and the doctor, unhinged by his desire for a woman he
cannot have, turns to a medicine older than his own.
'An imaginative tour de force and a considerable stylistic achieve-
ment. When it comes to pulling one into a world of his own
making, Gibson has few equals among his contemporaries.'
– *Time Out*

'A wild, poetic exhalation that sparkles and hoots and flies.'
– *The New Yorker*

'An extraordinary talent dances with perfect control
across hypnotic page.' – *Financial Times*

ISBN 1 899344 25 X – £7

The Sandman by Miles Gibson

*"I am the Sandman. I am the butcher in soft rubber gloves. I am the acrobat
called death.*
I am the fear in the dark. I am the gift of sleep..."
Growing up in a small hotel in a shabby seaside town, Mackerel
Burton has no idea that he is to grow up to become a slick and ruthless serial killer. A lonely boy, he amuses himself by perfecting his
conjuring tricks, but slowly the magic turns to a darker kind, and
soon he finds himself stalking the streets of London in search of
random and innocent victims. He has become The Sandman.
'A truly remarkable insight into the workings of a deranged mind:
a vivid, extraordinarily powerful novel which will grip you to the
end and which you'll long remember' – *Mystery & Thriller Guild*
'A horribly deft piece of work!" – Cosmopolitan
'Written by a virtuoso – it luxuriates in death with a Jacobean
fervour' – *The Sydney Morning Herald*
'Confounds received notions of good taste – unspeakable acts are
reported with an unwavering reasonableness essential to the
comic impact and attesting to the deftness of Gibson's control.'
– *Times Literary Supplement*

ISBN 1 899344 24 1 – £7

MAXIM JAKUBOWSKI

Because She Thought She Loved Me by Maxim Jakubowski

'He'll have to die.'

'Yes," I heard myself saying, sealing my fate...'

The course of true love doesn't run easy when your husband is a powerful pornographer who controls most of the shady side of the Internet. And when a tender love affair runs out of control, desperate measures are needed to stop the darkness engulfing its frantic protagonists.

Because She Thought She Loved Me offers a thrilling descent into the heart of sexual madness, moving in overdrive from London's West End, via the sinister private clubs of Paris, to the no-holds-barred illegal strip-joints of New York.

Maxim Jakubowski continues his daring exploration of the night-side of sex in a suspenseful tale full of memorable characters and sharp emotions.

ISBN 1 899344 27 6 – £7

It's You That I Want To Kiss by Maxim Jakubowski

They met among the torrid nightlife of Miami Beach, but soon they were running. From the Florida heat to rain-drenched Seattle, Anne and Jake blaze an unforgettable trail of fast sex, forbidden desires and sudden violence, pursued across America by a chilling psychopath.

Set against a backdrop of gaudy neon-lit American roadhouses and lonely highways, It's you that I want to kiss is a no-holds-barred rock 'n' roll road movie in print, in which every turn offers hidden danger, and where every stranger is a potential enemy. ISBN 1 899344 15 2 – £7.99

Life In The World Of Women

a collection of vile, dangerous and loving stories by **Maxim Jakubowski**

Maxim Jakubowski's dangerous and erotic stories of war between the sexes are collected here for the first time.

'Demonstrates that erotic fiction can be amusing, touching, spooky and even (at least occasionally) elegant. Erotic fiction seems to be Jakubowski's true metier. These stories have the hard sexy edge of Henry Miller and the redeeming grief of Jack Kerouac. A first class collection.' – Ed Gorman, *Mystery Scene* (USA)

ISBN 1 899344 06 3 – £6.99

The Do-Not Press
Fiercely Independent Publishing

Keep in touch with what's happening at the cutting edge of independent British publishing.

Join The Do-Not Press Information Service and receive advance information of all our new titles, as well as news of events and launches in your area, and the occasional free gift and special offer.

Simply send your name and address to:
The Do-Not Press (Dept. SoS)
PO Box 4215
London
SE23 2QD
or email us: thedonotpress@zoo.co.uk

There is no obligation to purchase and
no salesman will call.

Visit our regularly-updated Internet site:
http://www.thedonotpress.co.uk

Mail Order

All our titles are available from good bookshops, or (in case of difficulty) direct from The Do-Not Press at the address above. There is no charge for post and packing. (NB: A postman may call.)